MELANCHOLY SPRING

Holidaying on a cruise liner, Stella Bardon joins a 'Castaway Afternoon' to an uninhabited island. Later, having taken a stroll, she finds the boat has left without her. She remembers the lone yachtsman she had been surprised to see at the other end of the island, and he returns her to the liner in his yacht. From then on, Stella's search for the love that has been awakened in her takes her to the English Lake District, where they meet again . . .

Books by Lloyd Peters
in the Linford Romance Library:

ROSE ON THE PILLOW

LLOYD PETERS

MELANCHOLY SPRING

Complete and Unabridged

LINFORD
Leicester

First published in Great Britain in 1987

First Linford Edition
published 2003

British Library CIP Data

Peters, Lloyd
    Melancholy spring.—Large print ed.—
Linford romance library
    1. Love stories
    2. Large type books
    I. Title
    823.9'14 [F]

ISBN 1–8439–5054–5

Published by
F. A. Thorpe (Publishing)
Anstey, Leicestershire

Set by Words & Graphics Ltd.
Anstey, Leicestershire
Printed and bound in Great Britain by
T. J. International Ltd., Padstow, Cornwall

This book is printed on acid-free paper

1

Stella Bardon strolled, ankle deep, through the gentle surf, kicking the water occasionally with a sense of glorious freedom. She could have been the only person in the whole world; just herself, the ocean and the island.

Her backward glance over her shoulder spoiled that illusion, as she saw the cruise liner *Southern Princess*, anchored about a mile offshore, a graceful, white carving in the blue haze of the afternoon heat. She remembered the light-hearted banter of the younger males on board about her being a Girl Friday and maybe finding a Man Friday on the island. Details of this trip to the island had been billed on the ship's notice board as a 'Castaway' afternoon on an uninhabited island. Thinking it would be fun she had decided to join the party. It would be a change from sun bathing and swimming, enjoyable as those pastimes were.

Together with a few ship's officers and stewards they had landed at a small beach; and after refreshments some passengers went bathing, whilst others lay about on the white soft sand. Some, like herself, had decided to take a stroll. The others were exploring inland, but Stella had preferred to take her gentle exercise by the ocean's edge. As she strolled along the beach upon which she had landed and the other 'castaways' were gradually lost to sight, she was surprised to see how far she had come, but it was so soothing and peaceful letting her body and mind drift on. The sun was hot and high; and she was glad of her white, wide-brimmed hat, matching in colour her sleeveless top and short, squash-type skirt.

The island, as far as she could judge, appeared to be about a mile long, flat for about three quarters of its length, when the ground then rose gradually to form a small hill or ridge at the

2

end towards which she was moving. Its vegetation consisted principally of palms, umbrella pines and scrub grass.

Stella decided to ascend to the top of the hill, linger a while and rest, enjoying whatever view there was before returning to rejoin the main party. Perhaps, she mused, it was because she had been born and still lived in a hilly district of England that she was so curious to see what lay beyond the top of this relatively small eminence.

It was, however, with some reluctance that she left the cooling shallows and crossed the beach, the sand hot to her feet. The gentle slope she was ascending was sparsely covered with small pines, which latter also formed a dark coxcomb along the crest of the hill, silhouetted against the azure sky. As she neared the top a welcome light breeze began to fan her face and she paused at a gap between the trees, scanning the prospect below. Absolute astonishment held her motionless.

Below, a short distance off a small,

half-moon shaped beach, a light blue yacht, sails furled, lay quietly at anchor. There was a round, dark object amongst the million sun stars dancing on the water; it was someone swimming towards the beach. A knowledgeable enough swimmer herself she recognised the effortless action of the free style. As she continued to watch a man rose from the water.

As he came up the beach towards her, moving with the same easy action that had characterised his swimming, she saw that he was dark-haired, tautbodied and muscular, though not overly so. His skin was bronzed to a shade of gold, she imagined his age would be about thirty-three.

This side of the ridge sloped much more steeply than that she had ascended and she gazed down as the man made for a rough, canvas topped shelter, situated almost immediately below her. Stella knew she ought to move away, but she was powerless to do so; only when he had disappeared from sight would the spell be broken. But what if he should see her? She shrank inwardly at the thought.

He did see her, glancing upwards when he was a few yards from the shelter. What had caught his attention, she didn't know — perhaps the white of her outfit? They stared at each other — his glance one of sheer amazement as he paused, rigid in mid-stride. Just for a fraction of time they were immobile, like tabloid wax figures.

With a very real physical effort she stepped backwards, and in some confusion hurried back down the ridge towards the long stretch of beach.

As she regained the beach, she slowed down, beginning to recover a little from the surprise of seeing someone else, on what was supposed to be an uninhabited island. Had he put in there for repairs, after a storm? Was he a round-the-world yachtsman resting for a while? She shrugged mentally, then glanced backwards, part of her hoping that he might have been curious enough to follow her. In the few moments that she had seen his face fully, he had appeared handsome.

Stella sighed, as she left the sand and waded on through the shallows once more. Pausing only to put on her sandals, she struck out across the corner of the island, making for the area of beach where she and the rest of the party had been landed. It seemed very quiet, no voices, no sign of anyone. As she reached her goal, she gasped with shock; the beach was empty, the rest of the party nowhere to be seen. There was no launch swinging quietly and comfortingly at anchor, just a few empty, discarded cans and a multitude of footprints. The only sign of life was the gently waving group of palms, with the more stolid umbrella pines looking on. She shouted. Maybe her erstwhile companions had all drifted into the interior of the island; but she knew it was a vain hope. They were not there. The launch had gone and that meant that they had gone too.

Only the *Southern Princess* lay exactly where it had been. She stood at the edge of the ocean, then waded in, as if that would bring the ship nearer to her. Then came the wild idea of swimming back to the ship. She dismissed the idea; she was a good swimmer, but that would be tantamount to suicide. She began to wave frantically, her mind steadier after the initial shock of finding herself left behind. Was it possible she had been away so long? It hadn't seemed that long since she'd left the main party, but obviously it must have been. Surely they must have realised she was not aboard. Would they come back for her? Anger seized her. Why the hell couldn't they have waited a little while longer or searched for her? She hadn't been all that far away.

Then doubts came to haunt her. Perhaps they hadn't noticed she wasn't aboard the launch. Perhaps they would not discover her absence until some time after the liner had sailed again.

They might even think she'd fallen overboard. Shocked and deeply anxious, she stared across the water at the ship — so near and yet so far. If they didn't return for her, she was going to be left all alone on this island.

Suddenly she remembered the man at the other end of the island — the man with the yacht! She wasn't alone. Instantly hope and optimism flared. She would ask for his help, tell him what had happened. But then another fear struck her. What if he had set sail already? Perhaps he had only been making a brief stop?

Stella began to run back towards the long straight beach and some ten minutes later saw her own previous footprints, made as she had left the water to cross the sand and climb up the ridge — calm, carefree footprints, wandering idly. Perhaps even now, she thought, someone on the liner had binoculars trained on the island, on her, watching her undignified rush along the sands, no longer a sophisticated woman of the world, but a red-faced and dishevelled one.

She stumbled up the incline to the ridge top, looked over the edge and gasped in sheer relief; the yacht still lay at anchor. But of the man there was no sign. Was he on board? From her high position she could still clearly see the *Southern Princess*, but the water between it and the island remained empty. No search party had as yet set out. She must get help and it could only come from the man she now sought.

Immediately below her was the shelter which she had seen previously. Stella leaned over and called out, her voice like the cry of a gull in the wind. If he didn't appear, she would have to find some way down to the beach below. She shouted more urgently, this time directing her voice at the canvas top.

He appeared, holding a cloth around his waist. He looked around, obviously unsure where the sound had come from. Then he looked upwards and saw her.

'Oh thank God,' she breathed. Then: 'Excuse me, I'm sorry to bother you.' It sounded so silly, as if she were about to ask the way to a street in some city.

'What the hell are you doing here again?' His voice was deep — American, with an edge of irritation to his astonishment.

The words tumbled out of her, in her hurry to obtain his assistance. 'Please, will you help me?' she called down to him. 'I've been left behind. The boat's left without me. When I got back to the other beach they'd gone. I'm stranded here on the island. The ship may leave without me. I don't think they've realised yet that I'm missing.' Her voice sounded cracked and dry with her fear. She didn't know whether to laugh or cry. What an idiotic situation she'd got herself into.

He continued to stare up at her. Her second appearance had obviously surprised him more than she would have expected.

'I remembered seeing you here,' she

went on, 'I wondered if you could help me. I . . . I don't know what else to do.'

He nodded. 'Sure. I'll do what I can. What d'you say the name of your ship is?'

'The *Southern Princess*. Oh, thank you!' She sighed with relief.

'O.K. Now you stay here — keep an eye on your ship. If you see a boat coming in, give me a shout — right? I'll see if I can raise them on my transmitter.'

Stella nodded, feeling happier already. His regard lingered on her for a few moments more, before he turned away and made towards the yacht. She watched him, noting his easy walk, the curving muscles over the ends of his shoulders. No doubt he was thinking that if she hadn't spent so much time on her first visit to that part of the island, she wouldn't have missed her boat. It was quite true, she had to admit, that she had lingered a minute or two in admiration, but it had also been in surprise at seeing him there at all. Stella turned away, scanning the water between the island and the *Southern Princess*. No craft was to be seen heading in her direction.

After a few minutes, the American emerged and signalled her to come down to the water's edge. He stepped into the dinghy at the yacht's side and rowed towards her.

As the dinghy grounded, she gazed anxiously at him as he jumped from the boat.

'All right, Miss English,' his smile extended to his eyes. 'You're saved. They hadn't noticed your absence. I told them I'll take you back. You *are* English, aren't you?' His hazel, predominantly brown eyes were submitting her to a searching gaze.

'Yes . . . from the North of England.' She smiled back at him. 'It's very kind of you. I'm sorry for all the trouble I'm causing.'

He gave a slight shrug of the shoulders, a closed spreading of his lips.

'No problem.' He gestured towards

the beach. 'These places look O.K. in travel brochures, but they're not the kind of place where you'd want to spend the rest of your life.'

Getting into the dinghy, she wondered how long he'd been on the island himself. Certainly it was not just an overnight stop; the shelter on the beach was evidence of that — unless some other seafarer had erected it.

Her companion began to pull away from the shore, heading for his yacht, and Stella, now that her fear of being stranded on the island was gone, was better able to take stock of him. As she'd thought earlier, he'd be about thirty-five, his thick dark hair damp from the water and inclined to curl at his forehead. For the most, his was a serious, unsmiling face, but crinkles at the corners of his eyes could indicate occasional humour, or perhaps a constant narrowing against sun and sea glare. A little of each, she decided. There was a covering of dark hairs across his shoulders and chest, which could not hide the play of muscles as he pulled on the oars. On the beach, she recalled, he had towered over her; he must be at least six foot two.

They reached the yacht, and he helped Stella aboard. It was much larger than it had appeared from the beach. The name on the stern read *Fair Wind*. She sat in the cockpit watching him as he moved about the deck with a practised ease. She felt the craft swing as the anchor came up. The sails fluttered and filled, and the boat gathered way.

Her rescuer sat in the stern a few feet away from her, the tiller held lightly under his hand, eyes narrowed against the brightness. Stella wondered about him. Did it matter? She would never see him again. She watched the small beach and the ridge behind it fall astern; a small incident in her life had come and was almost gone.

Stella gestured back towards the island, smiling apologetically.

'I'd no idea you were there. I didn't

mean to intrude; they told us the island was uninhabited.'

'Time they updated their information system then.' He didn't look at her, but the merest lengthening of his mouth softened any brusqueness.

'It was my own fault really. I became lost in the beauty of the place. It's so quiet and peaceful.'

'A bit careless of them though, to leave you behind?' His glance lingered a fraction this time.

'I suppose so, but it must be difficult for them to keep an eye on everyone.' But in a way she couldn't help being glad it had happened; the incident had added an extra tinge of excitement to the day — the excitement of meeting this man, sitting only a few feet away from her. She realised that she didn't want the journey with this attractive man to be over too soon. Not one of the men on board the liner had excited her so much as this man had — and on so short an acquaintance. She was curious to find out more about him.

Turning to him she said:

'I suppose I gave you a shock, appearing so suddenly like that — over the hill top?'

The American nodded, a glint of wry humour in his hazel eyes. 'You surely did. Darn it! There was I, on a piece of God's earth one mile by a half, thinking that at last I'd got away from everything — that I was totally alone — and suddenly there's this face, under a white hat, staring at me.'

Stella laughed sympathetically.

'I can understand how you felt. I'd marked out that ridge as the limit of my afternoon stroll. I suppose I was curious to see what was on the other side.'

'I didn't expect to see you again after you'd disappeared from the ridge. I went up there myself — saw the liner — guessed you were from it. You did me good though. A man can be too much alone.' He surveyed her for a moment. 'And what state in England d'you come from?'

'County,' she corrected gently. 'They're called counties in England.'

He shrugged. 'O.K. Miss School-marm. Which county then?'

'Yorkshire. It's the largest in England and some of it is hilly and wet. Have you been to England?'

He looked up at the sail, 'No, but I once knew someone from there.'

She wondered what had happened to him in the past. A broken affair? A business deal gone wrong? He'd mentioned getting away from everything. Had he meant 'running away' from something? Judging by the yacht — if it was indeed his — he was wealthy. It was comfortable, big and modern and he had a look of success about him.

'Where does the liner head for next?' This time his eyes were directly upon her, his voice breaking in upon her thoughts. She hoped she hadn't been staring too openly.

'Las Palmas and then we sail for home.' There was a sigh in her words.

'You're not looking forward to going

home?' She felt that he in turn was observing her closely.

She shook her head. 'Not really. I've enjoyed the trip and a fortnight isn't long enough.'

'Where have you been?'

'Oh, Gibraltar, Faro, Tangier, Madeira, Las Palmas.' She decided to be bold. 'And you?'

He shrugged, looking away. 'Oh, just drifting, stopping where I felt like it. That's what I'd meant to do anyway, but I had to put in here.' He gestured back at the island. 'Steering trouble. I've fixed it, but somehow or other the place got to me and I'm still here.' His mouth widened ruefully. 'It's peaceful — too quiet, maybe. You get to thinking.' Though she waited he remained silent and she wondered what he'd been thinking about; there'd been a trace of sadness in his voice.

Stella relaxed, her back up against the yacht's coaming. The sun was pleasantly hot, the seabreeze cooling and by her side she had a handsome, kindly stranger. For a few moments she dreamed . . . about the two of them . . . in love . . . the boat taking them wherever they wished, to fashionable resorts or quiet islands. Ashore, on the arm of her escort, she would be the envy of every other woman. Then reality forced itself upon her, her eyes telling her that the *Southern Princess* was becoming larger. They were getting closer.

The American's eyes were just slipping away from her face as she looked round at him. His expression in profile was serious — even stern. He was a stranger and he would remain a stranger to her. She didn't even know his name.

'Have you set a time limit to your drifting?' she asked.

'No. I'm able to please myself now.'

He *must* be wealthy! How marvellous to be able to have no regard for time or work; and yet he didn't appear to be particularly happy.

'But I guess *you'll* have to return by a

certain date?' His eyes seemed to envelop her, blotting out the rest of the world.

'Yes,' she sighed, 'then all this will be a memory — a dream, as if I'd never been anywhere, with only photographs to remind me.' She was somewhat surprised when, at her mention of photographs, his gaze sharpened and concentration lines formed on his forehead.

'It's possible, you know, to tire even of this.' He swept the horizon with his hand.

She looked at the white foam spreading from the bows of the yacht, as the slap and rush of the ocean passed them. Did all this have to end so quickly? 'Oh, I suppose so,' she agreed, then smiled, 'but I'm sure I could put up with it for a long time.' She wrinkled her nose. 'Where I come from the weather is often dismal and cloudy. Even in the summer it can be depressing. It's something to do with the hills I think.'

'And what is your job back home?'

Stella pushed the hair back from her face, then fenced with her eyes at him.

'Guess!'

He bent forward to adjust a sheet before he answered, then looked at her sideways out of the crinkling corners of his eyes, his gaze roaming her face. Arrows of pleasure struck her.

'Well,' he drawled, 'you're not a motor mechanic. That's for sure!' Briefly his eyes left her face to take note of the rest of her; it was like the switching off of a lamp. Brief as his gaze had been, it produced a surge of sensuality throughout her body. The lamp shone again. 'A model?'

Stella laughed. It was very flattering and nice to hear, even if he didn't mean it.

'No, but I would have liked to have been one.' She wasn't fashionably thin enough.

He continued to regard her with just a faint increase of interest. 'I know — what about in a library?' Before she could complete the short shake of her head he went on, 'all right, don't tell me, you're a woman airline pilot or something?'

Stella chuckled, her summer blue eyes matching the sea behind her. 'I'm afraid it's nothing as glamorous as that. I'm a teacher in a kindergarten school; four to seven year olds. They also gave me the job of school swimming instructress.'

'Ah! So no doubt you ran your professional eye over my style earlier today. Did I come up to standard?'

There was a challenging, provocative gleam in his regard. He certainly had come up to her standard. Ten more minutes and they would be parted for ever.

'You'll be in the next Olympic Games,' she told him.

He smiled slowly with his lips closed, then eased one of the sheets again and looked forward under the sails, keeping on course towards the *Southern Princess*.

His wasn't a finely cut face, she thought. He had seen some life and it showed, but she could guess at a warm personality lying beneath the surface. He seemed more relaxed with her now. She decided it would be nice to know his name, and extended her hand to him.

'It's a bit late now and not that it matters much, but I'm Stella Bardon.'

Just for a second he hesitated, then his large brown hand enclosed her small paler one.

'Nice to have you aboard, Stella.'

Thoughtfully he repeated her name. 'Stella — that's a nice feminine name. Means a star if I remember rightly.'

She nodded, thinking that he made her name sound something special.

'I'm Carey — Carey Ganton. Can't say that means anything. You're given a name and that's it.' He let go of her hand.

Carey. Yes, it suited him. He was worldly wise, he'd made his way. He was educated, but not too smooth; yet he was a man carrying doubts and for some reason not at ease with himself. She wanted to find out more about him, conscious that they were drawing ever nearer to the cruise ship. A feeling was growing in her, astonishing her by its strength. How could it be so in such a short time? She tried to calm herself, to make herself sound politely and carelessly interested, no more than that.

'And what do you do . . . er . . . ' She hesitated a fraction over his name, 'Carey . . . when you're not sailing? Have you any other interests?'

He glanced ahead before answering, making sure they were still on course. 'I make my money out of yachts, selling them. But I like old cars too. I collect them . . . convertibles, that sort of thing. Those and sailing keeps me from thi . . . ' He broke off, looking away from her, concentrating on helming the yacht, concentrating too hard, Stella thought. He'd been about to say it kept him from thinking, of that she was certain. Why should he need something to keep him from thinking? About what?

He spoke again. 'You mentioned Las Palmas. Is it possible that you were going to be presented to someone because you'd won a competition . . . something to do with boats?' The dancing water was reflected in the humorous gaze of his eyes.

Stella stared at him, dumbfounded. This must be the most crazy half day of her life.

'How . . . how d'you know that?' she managed at last.

His look lingered on her; he was quite obviously enjoying her astonishment. Then taking her hand he placed it on the tiller, exactly where his had been.

'Keep it just there. No need to worry — she'll stay on course.'

Stella stared apprehensively at his back, as without saying another word he disappeared into the cabin. For a few moments she felt the thrill of riding and guiding this beautiful piece of man's creation over the water. But it was with some relief, however, that she saw Carey emerge from the cabin to take over control of *Fair Wind* again. But first he provided her with one more huge surprise by handing her a photograph.

The photograph was of herself. It had been taken very early in the year and was one she'd had made specially for a competition she'd entered. To her delight she'd won, the prize being a cruise and a presentation to the chairman of the yacht company, to take place at an hotel in Las Palmas. She stared at Carey, searching his face for some clue:

'It's the one I sent along with my competition entry, but I . . . I mean . . . how did you . . . ?'

'First,' he interrupted gently, 'let me apologise for not being in Las Palmas at the Lawns Hotel yesterday to meet you. But I'm sure you managed all right without me.'

Stella was beginning to understand.

'The Sunside Yacht Company,' he prompted.

'You're not the . . . ?'

'Yes, the chairman of that company. It was my company that featured in the competition.' He offered his hand. 'Congratulations anyhow. At least you've been presented to the chairman, even if it was a day late. Unfortunately the repairs I mentioned before delayed me.'

Stella let her hand remain lost in his.

'Perhaps it was just as well you were delayed or I might have still been on the island.' She still felt bemused.

They were close enough to the liner now, to see people lining the rails watching their approach, binoculars trained on them. Stella supposed word had spread about her being left behind on the island.

She threw a quick glance at Carey. Her heart was running away from common sense and reason. Those sails billowing out above her, heralded a message which only she understood.

She too was filled, but with a sudden, overwhelming love for the man returning her to the *Southern Princess* . . . a man to whom she was going to have to say 'thank you' and 'goodbye' for ever in a few minutes' time. It was insane, stupid, but true. She was in love.

As one in a dream, she saw him furl the sails and the boat lost way through the water, then he returned to the cockpit. He had a preoccupied, distant air. She was aware now of the vibration of the engine and they began to curve towards the boarding platform and ladder. She felt sad and helpless as she watched him concentrating on bringing his yacht alongside.

Carey threw a couple of fenders over the side and a few minutes later Stella felt *Fair Wind* nudge the liner's platform, to lie dipping and rising on the slight swell . . . a porpoise paying its respects to a whale.

'Well, this is it, Stella, home again!'

She rose at the sound of his voice and held on to the safety wire. Damn those people looking down at them. She put out her hand.

'Thanks for everything, Carey. So kind of you. You certainly rescued a maiden in distress.' Oh, what could she tell him through her eyes?

For the second time in the last half hour he held her hand.

'No trouble. I wasn't doing anything in particular. Just remember next time to stick with the party ... and congratulations again.'

Impulsively she stretched upwards and touched Carey's cheek with her lips, felt the sweat, the warmth, the masculinity of the between-shaves skin.

'Goodbye,' she whispered.

His hand remained holding hers until that of a steward took over and she felt the stage beneath her feet. Misty-eyed she put her foot on the first step of the ladder.

'Are you all right, Miss?' said the steward. 'Anything I can get for you? It must have been a frightening experience.'

'It was at first, but I'm fine now thanks,' she said, smiling briefly at him. She didn't want to talk; the transition from Carey's presence to that of others was an anticlimax.

At the top of the gangway, she ran the gauntlet of curious questions and was glad when she managed to get away on the pretext of being tired and wanting to rest. All she wanted just now was to reach the quiet and privacy of her cabin.

Once there she pressed her face to the porthole seeing the blue-hulled yacht drawing ever further away. The figure at the tiller — did he turn once and look back? She thought so. She put her hand out and waved, but he wouldn't see it of course. It would be far too small in all those rows of similar holes in the slab-sided, metal mountain she was on. She began to wish that her cabin had been on the other side so that she would have been unable to see him go. That way, she would have been spared the terrible ache now gnawing at her. Private tears ran unheeded down her face. Could love really have come so swiftly? Piercing her heart so easily? Now she knew. She waited until the white sails disappeared in the distance, around the far end of the island, taking a man called Carey out of her life. No doubt he had forgotten about her already. She had just been a short interruption in his wealthy, easy-going lifestyle. Turning away into the cabin again she told herself that she must be realistic. Life could be cruel. She would just have to forget him.

Later Stella showered, hoping that the water running away the stains of the day would at the same time drown memories of that afternoon. Afterwards she felt refreshed physically, but her mind persisted with its imagery. She ordered tea in her cabin, sat on her bed sipping it, recalling how Carey had seemed almost to flinch as she had kissed him on the cheek, her impression that he was a man with some inner conflict. She remembered too the slow-growing glint of humour in his eyes, which she had longed to fan into laughter to relieve the stern repose of his face.

Why, oh why hadn't she asked for his address so that she would have still had some connection with him, however tenuous? Why hadn't she given him her telephone number, *her* address? She knew of girls who could have done that easily, light-heartedly, but not her. Perhaps the whole thing had happened too quickly; she had been so anxious and worried at one stage, then Fate had taken her, romantically speaking, by surprise. She hadn't been prepared for the encounter with the American . . . with Carey. Of course it must have been a similar experience for him, the difference being that *she* had fallen in love.

That evening she was invited to dine at the Captain's table. He listened with great interest to her story. When she finished he smiled comfortingly and said:

'Of course we knew you were missing; we found out almost immediately. The boat was just about to return for you when we had a message from this yachting fellow — an American — to say that he was bringing you over. I'm sorry if you were worried. It can't have been very nice for you, alone on the island even for a short time. I've had a word with the Officers concerned.'

'Please don't be cross with them on my account.' Stella touched the full-braided sleeve gently. 'I shouldn't have strayed, and anyway I wasn't alone all the time. I did have some company.'

'Ah yes, of course. Not the knight on a white horse — but an American in a blue yacht.' His eyes gleamed kindly, knowingly, then he added admiringly, 'and a darned fine yacht from what I saw of it. Wouldn't mind that myself.'

Nor I the man in it, thought Stella sadly.

For the rest of the evening she had to put up with a lot of teasing and envious remarks from members of her own sex. The general consensus of opinion amongst the women who had witnessed her return was that Carey had been something special.

During the remaining days of the cruise, she flung herself into every activity, games, dances, competitions, going ashore at every port of call, but to no avail. When she least expected it Carey's face would appear before her eyes, sometimes so vividly that she almost spoke aloud to him. She found herself searching the faces of the male tourists, trying to find the one face she wanted to see again, knowing that it was madness, telling herself to get a grip.

On the last night on board she fell asleep holding the pillow tightly to her, just as Carey's lips were closing on hers, lowering himself to crush her to the hot sand on that lonely island.

2

Back home in Halton in Yorkshire — a town on the edge of the moors — Stella was gathered up into the routine of school again. The young faces gazed into her tanned one, inquisitive about her holiday, giggling and wide-eyed when she told them about places she had visited.

The first week back was the hardest to bear, Stella wishing that she had never gone on that holiday and never met the American called Carey Ganton. But then during the following weeks her heartache became just a little less acute as the glamour and attraction of the holiday faded under the influence of the harsher and duller surroundings.

One evening with a dull sky and a light drizzle falling Stella sat alone in a restless and brooding mood. Television, radio, books held no interest for her. As one memory began to fade another one intruded. The main reason for her being glad to go on the holiday after winning it had been the leaving home of her sister Pauline nearly a year before. Very early in their lives they had been adopted by a childless couple and cared for and brought up wonderfully. But then, when well into their teens, they had decided to flee the parental nest and be independent and live by themselves. Stella being two years older had always taken it upon herself to mother and look after Pauline.

She remembered the shock she had had when Pauline announced that she was tired of the humdrum life in Halton and was going to Australia to find work. It had always been her wish to go there and perhaps join an airline as a stewardess.

Stella had been staggered, telling Pauline that she was crazy. Pauline had been adamant but had promised that she would write regularly and give Stella all her news.

The house had seemed empty when she had gone. Saddened and worried, Stella carried on living alone, each day looking eagerly for letters from her sister. They came at unequal intervals. She had found work in Sydney but was still hoping to fulfil her ambition and become an airline stewardess. But the tone of her letters was happy, and Stella was relieved and pleased. Then had come the chance to get herself on the cruise and forget her anxieties and loneliness. Away from the place where she and her sister had lived most of their lives.

And so she had gone on the holiday, seeing new sights, meeting new people and beginning to smile again. But a new scar had now formed over her heart — a scar of a different kind to that left by the leaving of her sister. For a cruelly brief period she had ridden a love star behind a man called Carey. Her eyes saw the calendar on the wall with its picture. It was April and springtime, but a melancholy spring for her.

In the middle of May she had a few days off from school and went up to Windermere in the English Lake district. One of her favourite places. She stayed in a farmhouse which took a few guests and was only about two miles from the lake itself.

Apart from it being one of her favourite beauty spots, Windermere lake had a special attraction for her. In a few months it would be her adversary and she wanted to have a look at it. Occasionally over the last few years she had entered for the swim across the lake held once a year at the end of July. She had crossed before but it didn't get any easier, though afterwards was worth all the effort and training. Sometimes the entrants were sponsored, the money going to a charity or some deserving cause.

Stella had decided to go ahead with her plans to attempt the swim again — preparation for it would help to keep her from dwelling on the man called Carey with his blue-hulled yacht.

Parking her car near Bowness — the busy little resort near the southern end of the lake — she made for the path running along the latter's eastern side. It was a fresh English spring day with lightweight white clouds queuing up over the surrounding hills, then scudding swiftly over as if not daring to offend the sun.

She glimpsed the ferry making its unhurried passage across the lake. A couple of miles inland from the other side was the old village of Hawkshead with its lovely old Inns. She remembered dining in one of them — in a corner next to the very old wooden frame of a many-squared window — the latter dated sixteen-sixty-three. Stella had thought of the eyes so long gone that had looked through it.

Turning away from the lake she continued along the path by the small meadow, the clumps of yellow daffodils nodding as they had for the famous poet; then through an iron gate which brought her near some chandlers' shops and a boatyard. She could see the masts of yachts moored at the pontoons and the flutter of a white sail as one moved out into the lake. She decided that she would face the sun for a few minutes then have a coffee in Bowness. Afterwards she would make her way up to Ambleside at the northern end of the lake where the swim took place and perhaps have lunch there.

Stella leaned against the rail looking across the lines of boats moving gently at their ropes. An ideal day especially for the sailing yachts.

One of the latter was just slipping out into the open water, stern on to her and beginning to bear away slightly to the right, making a course up lake. A mid summer blue hull — tall masts, its size more apparent as it became side on to her. Stella screwed her eyes. No! What she had just seen on the yacht's stern could not be possible! Nevertheless the gold coloured letters continued to reflect in the late morning sun the name *Fair Wind*. A man stood at the tiller his back to her; darkish hair and dark-armed under a white peak cap, white-shirted.

Gripping the rail Stella leaned far over it, straining her eyes. It couldn't be. It must be another yacht of the same name — same hull colour. The vessel she knew as *Fair Wind* had been left two thousand miles away near a sub tropical island. She continued to watch until it was hidden from sight before she moved.

Seated in the lounge of the nearest lakeside restaurant she stared over her coffee, seeing nothing. Her heart had suddenly transferred itself to her brain and was hammering down an excited beat. Her mind tried to tell her that even if it was the yacht *Fair Wind*, there was no guarantee that Carey was the man she had seen at the helm. She forced herself to think calmly. He could have sold it and the new owner had then brought it up to Windermere. Yes, of course that was it — the simple explanation. On leaving to pick up her car her rapid heart beats reaffirmed what she knew already — that she was still in love with the American.

Reaching Ambleside she parked her car then walked across the road to the shingle beach from where in two months' time she and other swimmers would be taken by boat to the other side and then swim back.

Stella gazed across the daunting expanse of water to a particular spot on the other side. Her stomach fluttered as she visualised herself and the others lined up in the cold water. Why did she do it? She was always glad when it was over. But paying her respects to the lake that day did not have the same interest as in other years. Her eyes kept straying into the far distance down lake. Several yachts were now out and the lake steamer from Bowness was approaching. But Stella wasn't looking for that. She was searching for a two-masted blue-hulled yacht called *Fair Wind*.

Deep inside herself she knew that she had to find out — put her mind at rest, even if it meant being bitterly disappointed.

She knew that she was taking it for granted that the yacht was being sailed to the northern end of the lake. Even if that were so it would be a few hours before it arrived.

The shops in the village held little attraction for her. She was just whiling away the time, her eyes straying to the water often. Someone was playing a banjo in one of them. A happy lighthearted tune serenading the spring day. Afterwards she stood on the shingle shore again to gaze down lake, cursing the fact that she hadn't a pair of binoculars with her.

There were several yachts which appeared to be coming her way but they were too far off to be able to distinguish their colours easily. Stella tried to force some logic into her disorderly thoughts. In the unlikely event that it was Carey just supposing he came ashore and they met again. What would she say to him? A cynical voice inside her dismissed the possibility of having to say anything at all. It would not matter. He would have forgotten all about her by now, probably wouldn't even recognise her. She glanced at her watch and was surprised to find that two hours had elapsed since she had left Bowness. A boat of the *Fair Wind's* size could she supposed make the passage in that time.

Her eyes returned to the lake. The sun was pleasantly warm now and the water had taken on the blue and white patchwork of the sky. Its effect was to deceive Stella's eyes into thinking that several yachts had become blue coloured. Shading her brow she continued to stare. One of them was indeed blue-hulled, she was certain. It was like looking at a picture and failing to see some object in the foreground. This object — the yacht — had stolen up upon her unnoticed. Taking her unawares. It had two masts, a touch of white near the stern. The American-Carey? It trailed a smaller boat.

When it was about two hundred yards away the yacht rounded up stern on to her. Again the name was clearly visible. She watched as the man on deck went forward, probably anchoring or mooring she guessed. Then he disappeared from sight into the yacht's interior. A few minutes later the man reappeared and climbed down into the small dinghy alongside. There was the strident sound of a small engine firing and then the dinghy turned away from the parent vessel.

Shading her eyes she gazed intently at the figure drawing nearer. It was Carey — she was sure. She wanted it to be and yet the prospect of meeting him again turned her insides to jelly. Just as she thought he would indeed land at her feet he veered slightly away to make for a small jetty to her left. His features were becoming ever more distinct and under the cap she saw the dark handsome face.

Stella made her way to the rear of the narrow beach, halted under a tree next to the pathway on to which the man she believed was Carey would step from the inner end of the jetty. The man she was now convinced was Carey came along it with long slow swinging strides. He was wearing a cream chunky sweater. Stella searched the face beneath the cap, unaware of herself moving closer to the jetty. If only he would take off the cap. She held her breath — concentrating.

It was! It was Carey! No doubt about it, coming along the wooden boards with a slow smile beginning to show. He must have seen her — recognised her. He seemed to be looking straight at her. He had remembered.

She paid no attention to the doors of a car being opened behind her at the roadside. He would hear her heart so near to bursting at the sight of him.

Suddenly he was abreast of her, then passed her, his hand outstretched to someone else. Her own half-raised and the joy turning to a terrible dismay. Yet even as she stood frozen looking after him he glanced backwards at her momentarily.

Stella became aware of a well-dressed man and a woman in front of a silver saloon. The man's hand was shaking the one which should have held hers. The woman dark haired — a little older than herself dressed in a fashionable spring velvet maroon trouser suit was being introduced to Carey. Then all three got into the car and were driven away, but not before Stella had observed Carey's over the shoulder glance at her again. The tinted glass stopped her from seeing his full expression.

She turned away feeling foolish, avoiding the faces of those people close by, and found a seat overlooking the water. She was miserable and felt let down. She had expected too much. The woman with whom Carey had driven off had been smart and wealthy looking. Stella glanced down at her jeans, heavy knitted jumper and her faded white training shoes.

She continued to sit and stare out over the lake. He had noticed her, twice he had glanced at her. Definitely his memory had been stirred. No doubt he would have shrugged it out of his mind by now and be enjoying the company of the dark haired woman. Stella hunched herself up on the seat, arms around her knees, and stared disconsolately at the yacht *Fair Wind* gently moving in the swell from other craft. Suddenly it occurred to her that Carey would have to return sometime to the boat. But when? It could be hours, even tomorrow. She shrank inside herself at the thought of how foolish she had made herself look, thinking that his smile and extended hand had been for her. Really she ought to collect her car and go home, she told herself. And yet something held her — made her remain — seated — hating herself for being so weak. Supposing he did come back. What was she going to do? Stand in his path like some star struck pop fan? Stella gazed morosely at the shingle in front of her.

From about her came the subdued noise of people and traffic and the quiet murmur of the water. She put her arm along the seat, hand propping her head, and turned so that she could see the end of the jetty. Just an hour then she would exercise her willpower and leave. Her eyelids drooped.

3

The voice came low, vibrant, and American from close by. 'Pardon me but didn't I see you earlier this afternoon — over by the jetty there.'

It was a dream Stella thought and didn't want to wake up. Past her hand she saw Carey's face. He was crouched down on his haunches, eyes level with hers. She sat up, her eyes still locked with his — disbelieving.

His steady hazel stare from under the shade of his cap held a questioning amusement. He took it off. 'We seem fated to meet by water. You're Stella — the girl lost on the island. I'm Carey, remember? My yacht's over there.' He pointed at it.

She sat up, instinctively arranging her hair. 'Carey!' The name was heaven, and to be talking to him. 'But I thought you — I mean, I saw you getting into a car.' It was no use pretending that she had not been waiting for him near the jetty. He had seen her.

'You did. I had some business to attend to and as soon as I had finished it I decided that it was too nice a day to spend inside.' He straightened and came to sit next to her.

'But the last time I saw you you were going back to that island.'

A growing warm amusement showed. 'And the last time I saw you, you were on that liner — far away from here,' he countered.

She looked away, otherwise, she would not string two sensible words together. 'But this is England — I live here. I thought that you would have gone back to America.'

'No, I felt that I did not want to return just then.' He paused, his eyes in the past, remembering something, then went on, 'It was you who gave me the idea of coming to England. It was something I'd meant to do but never got round to doing. Too busy I guess.'

'Oh, what did I say to influence you?' She lost herself in his eyes again. The day was becoming more beautiful and exciting by the minute.

His shoulders lifted slightly. 'You were all a part of England right there in the middle of the ocean. I decided to follow. Took me a while longer.' A smile played at his mouth corners.

How wonderful, she thought, if he had said that it was because he wanted to follow her and meet her again.

Carey turned on the seat until he was facing her fully. 'But what brings you to Windermere? Are you on holiday again?'

She explained how on this occasion it was to do with her swimming in the lake and saw the astonishment and admiration in his expression.

'You mean to tell me you swim in that? Hell, it looks cold enough for icebergs.' He touched her elbow; it was like an electric shock hitting her. 'Come on Stella, I'd like you to show me whereabouts.'

She pointed out in the distance where she and the others would start from.

'And why do you do it, Stella?'

She laughed shortly, carelessly, thrilling at his use of her name. 'I suppose a challenge — something to aim for. But also it's a way of getting money for some cause. People sponsor us. If you complete the swim the money collected goes to whatever charity or cause you've chosen.'

'And what have you chosen?' His eyes probed her face again.

'Oh, probably as before, a children's society — that sort of thing.'

'You like children?' He seemed to be very close to her and the rest of the world had suddenly become muted. 'Even though you're with them in your work?'

She was pleased that he had remembered. 'Oh yes, and I suppose because we were adopted — my sister and I — when we were young. We were happy. It's one way of ensuring that others get the chance of finding a home and love.' Now she wanted another love — his love, and his children.

'And is your sister a teacher also?' he inquired.

'No, she left home a few months ago. She's hoping to be an airline steward-ess. She's in Australia just now. I miss her very much.'

'I know how you feel, Stella.' The sad regret in his words caused her to recall his serious and withdrawn demeanour on the island. Perhaps he too had been trying to get over a trouble. She waited for some explanation.

He looked away across the lake. 'We were going to be married.'

It was Stella's turn to utter a sound of sympathy.

He glanced at her. 'No — no, it was for the best. In fact I didn't want to marry her.'

She was intrigued and puzzled and also relieved that he was not married. 'But you loved her?' It felt strange to be discussing something in his private life.

He faced her. 'No, I never loved her. It was a great relief when I was free of her. How I got mixed up with her I'll never know.' He laughed shortly without humour.

So that was it; a breakup not a bereavement. But a man like this; attractive, rich and handsome, would run the risk of getting involved anytime. There was a warning there for herself. If ever she got to know him better would there come a time when he would be telling someone else that he was glad that he had escaped marriage with her? She became aware that he was addressing her again.

'How long are you here for, Stella?'

She sighed. 'Just the day.' Then added wistfully, 'When the weather's like this I wish I could stay longer.' And with you forever, she added silently.

'Ah, a pity. Well, how about joining me for a sail in *Fair Wind*? She's restless to be on the move again.' His gaze lingered for a few seconds on

Stella. 'And we're not exactly strangers are we?'

They were not. She smiled and accepted in happy agreement. She must live this time with him to the full. It was more than likely that she would never see him again. Suddenly she remembered her car. 'I've left my car across the road.'

He smiled and shrugged. 'No problem. I'll bring you back here. Mine's down at Bowness.'

It was only when Carey helped her aboard the yacht that Stella began to realise that it really had happened, and she was actually with him on *Fair Wind* again. Carey set the sails and they drifted off down lake, and Stella thought of the last time she had been on board. Then she was being taken back to the liner thinking she would never see him again.

When he asked if she would like a drink she was glad — it would give her something to do with her hands. If not they might reach out of their own accord and paw him. He disappeared into the yacht's interior to reappear a short while later with a couple of sherries.

He sat down next to her. 'These will sharpen our appetites.' Were they going to eat together later, she wondered? They clinked glasses. 'To your successful swim, Stella,' he murmured, his eyes holding hers. 'When did you say it was?'

'The last day in July at six o'clock in the evening.' Was he thinking of watching? She put the possibility out of her mind. All that mattered was today.

Carey just nodded and was silent for a few minutes, then he gestured around him. 'You know, Stella, I'd no idea that the Lake District was so beautiful — everything about it.'

Did his glance linger again on her? Anything could happen on this magical day. 'Of course,' she pointed out, 'there are other lakes nearby — Coniston, Derwent-water, Ullswater.'

'You sound like a guide, Stella.' His

smile was provocative, his eyes, narrowed against the brightness, making lines at the corners of his eyes. 'You must show me those places some time.'

Stella's heart bounded, but she dare not allow herself to dwell too much on that. He could say it just in conversation and not really mean it. 'Just tell me when,' she laughed lightly. She would never forget the island. It was where she had fallen in love. Now she was seated next to the object of her love and he quite unaware of that emotion.

All too soon for Stella she saw that they were abreast of Bowness and very near to where she had first seen *Fair Wind* setting sail earlier that day.

Stella dreamed. Perhaps those people watching would think that she was Carey's wife, or a film star taking a break from location work and enjoying the company of the leading man. Was he going to take her back to her car now? She hoped not. Her day with him must not end yet, though it would have to sometime.

It was not to end at that point because after Carey had moored the yacht he said, 'I'm hungry now and I guess you will be. How about us finding a place to eat? It's only early — you don't have to go home yet do you?'

She certainly did not. If he had asked that at midnight it still would have been too soon.

'Right, we'll pick up my car and you can show me how good a guide you are.' His eyes enveloped her in a hazy world of just two people.

On shore again he took her hand and led her across the road to the car park. They stopped besides an open car the colour of the spring sky above. Stella recognized it as being a Rolls-Royce, long, low and with a sumptuous-looking white interior. He held the door open for her, and she sank into the softness of the leather seats.

As they eased away Carey glanced at her. 'Now, wherever you wish to go I'll take you.'

If he had seen the sudden darkening

of Stella's eyes he might have been surprised at her answer. Into his arms in the quietest part of the world. Buried in a fierce raging love embrace. Instead after a moment's thought she replied, 'Let's go to Hawkshead, Carey. It's an old world village across the other side of the lake — a few miles beyond it. I think you'll like it, it's pretty and the school that the poet Wordsworth went to is there. And the way to it is so lovely too, particularly at this time of the year. We can get the car ferry across. I'll show you.' She settled back as they cleared the car park.

'Can you eat there?' he asked.

'Oh yes, there's a couple of inns there — old ones. They're very quaint.'

'Sure then, let's go — sounds interesting.' He smiled that close-lipped smile of his.

In a few minutes they were clanking over the iron causeway on to the ferry, then came the curious sensation of the car moving over the water as they remained seated in it. Again Stella noticed that they and the car were the subject of scrutiny and she tried to look as if she were used to it. It must be like this for stars — anyone in the public eye, anyone famous. Let them think she was.

Ten minutes later and they were skirting the edge of the lake again for a while and then climbing and leaving it behind. It was marvellous, the breeze touching her hair and the car swishing along. Stella glanced once at her companion — rakish looking under the peaked yachting cap, his darkly handsome profile showing a calm contentment as he caressed the wheel. If only those hands would one day caress her.

On reaching Hawkshead they walked, she pointing out places and objects of interest. For most of the time Carey's hand rested lightly upon her waist — a delicious and nerve-tingling sensation. She was also proud at being accompanied by the tall, commanding, handsome figure of the American.

Soon they were stepping down into the warm and cosy sombreness of the White Swan Inn, all dark wood and beams, Stella smilingly warning Carey to duck his head at the entrance. She pointed out to him the old window near the corner seat.

Before their meal the champagne cork popped and Carey filled their glasses. 'To our coming together again, Stella,' and his eyes gleamed roguishly at her.

She drank to that. Would they ever come together in love? Her pride was gone where this man was concerned. Surely he must see that desire in her gaze. He would think her easy. 'I never thought of seeing you again, Carey.'

He laughed kindly, low voiced. 'You looked as if you'd seen a ghost when I spoke to you — you were dozing, I think.'

And dreaming of you, she thought. It struck her that she had heard him laugh for the first time in their relationship.

Humour remained in his eyes but a

seriousness now joined it, darkening his regard of her. It was as if some other memory had been touched by the spread of the first. 'The sight of you was so unexpected. It couldn't be, I thought, and yet you obviously knew me — and I you but . . . I just couldn't believe it.'

During the meal they chatted and Carey gave her a glimpse of his life in America. The stern features had relaxed and he spoke more freely. From their first encounter she understood that he had been seeking peace and solitude, leaving a hurtful period in his life behind. No wonder then that he had been wary of further intrusion into it. And had the story of repairs to the yacht just been an excuse not to attend the presentation in Las Palmas?

He refilled her glass as the shadows outside the inn became longer. She wanted to ask him something but was afraid of what his answer might be. After hesitation she took the plunge. 'When are you thinking of returning to

America?' She tried to keep her tone careless. She waited, masking that fear by pushing her plate aside, her eyes averted lest he should read what was in them.

Carey reached for his glass then cupped it between his hands. 'I've decided to stay in England. I've been looking at some property round here. Matter of fact that's what I was doing this morning.'

She met his eyes regarding her closely and thoughtfully across the table, her heart nearly stopped with the glorious excitement his words had stirred in her. 'Oh! How nice for you. I'm glad — it's such a beautiful part of England.' How barren and banal it sounded. Oh why couldn't he see the aura surrounding her which pulsated with 'I love you'? At least now she would have the chance to meet him again. 'I'll bet you're excited about it — I know I would be.'

Carey's gaze left her. 'Sure — sure I am. Looking forward to it. As you say,

Stella, it's a beautiful part of your country.' He didn't look excited and his tone had been matter of fact.

'And you'll be within easy distance of your yacht, Carey,' she pointed out.

Pleasure settled on his features at her mention of it. 'Yes, I'll be able to keep an eye on her.'

A stab of jealousy penetrated Stella at that pleasure. Damn the boat — keep an eye on me, her mind shouted at him. Aloud she asked, 'Are you living on board until you find a house?'

Carey gave a half smile. 'No. I guess it can be a bit lonely, so I'm staying at the Old Britannia Hotel until I clinch the deal on the house.'

'Oh, you've decided on one.'

He nodded. 'I think I've decided on the house I went to see this morning. I had only a quick look around — I think my mind was on where I'd seen you before, rather than on the house.' That was something anyway — better than nothing, she thought.

'I think it will do for me,' he

continued. 'It's got several features I like.' He paused, crinkling the sides of his eyes. 'That's Ambleside where I met you this morning?' Stella nodded smiling dreamily, entranced by his accent. 'Well, I'd say it's about a mile back towards Bowness — top side of the road. Stands back.'

'When I've moved in, Stella, you'll have to come and let me show you the place.' His gaze was like a space ray raking her mind.

'I'd love to, Carey.' That was the truth.

'There's just one or two things I want to have altered in the house — I have a few plans in mind.'

She prayed that his plans would include her also, and over coffee she gave way to her curiosity. 'What made you decide to settle in this area of England? I mean, I know it's got the lakes — all right for the boat, but . . .' She lifted her shoulders. He could have picked anywhere in the world.

Carey settled his cup in his saucer,

leaned his fore-arms on the table and smiled indulgently at her. 'Well for a start I guess I've got more English blood in me than you imagine. It's rather a romantic story. My father was a GI.' He must have seen the puzzled look on the face opposite. 'Short for Government Infantry in the second world war,' he explained. 'He was posted over here and met my mother who, believe it or not, came from near Windermere — I'm not just sure whereabouts, I may find out later. Anyway they fell for each other and he took her back to the States after the war.'

'You're right, Carey, it is romantic. And how wonderful you coming to live in the place where your mother met your father.' Would history repeat itself and romance blossom between Carey and herself?

It was getting dark outside. How soon the glorious day in Carey's company was passing. He must have noticed her glance through the window and mistaken its meaning.

'What time is the last ferry?' he asked.

'I think nine-thirty. I'm not sure.'

He glanced at his watch, a shadow of annoyance came and went. 'Forgive me, Stella, I'd no wish to make you late, it's just after nine now. I forgot that you have to drive back. How long will it take you?' His eyes had darkened with consideration for her.

She smiled his concern away. 'Oh, about two hours.'

'Maybe you'd better let me book you a room in my hotel.'

Part of her screamed to take his offer. He could go out of her life again if she did not. The other part won. 'It's very kind of you, Carey, but I've got to work tomorrow. I must get back.' It sounded unconvincing and somehow unsophisticated.

'All right, if you think you can manage.' He did not seem put out and called for the bill.

In the car with the hood up it was

warm and cosily luxurious.

For Stella there was the torturing delight of him barely a foot away from her — it might just as well have been a mile. Nevertheless it was a dream come true, cocooned in the darkness with the man she had thought lost to her forever.

They spoke occasionally, he caressing her senses with his deep vibrant voice, answering her curiosity about his country and also revealing other things about himself in doing so. There was the pull of the sea and foreign places as a Navy officer for a few years and then the founding of his yacht empire, his desire to collect and show cars again — the house he was thinking of purchasing, having a stable suitable for conversion to a showroom. Enthusiasm and excitement had edged his voice. A restless spirit was revealed to her.

Then sooner than she wished, Carey was turning the car alongside hers in the now deserted car park at Ambleside.

He switched off the engine then leaned across and said, 'Sure you won't let me take you back to my hotel, Stella? Separate rooms of course. You could start off early tomorrow.' His voice was soft, persuasive and very close in the quiet of the car. Had there been a gentle hint of mockery?

She smiled at him in the semi darkness, glad of it to hide her conflicting emotions. 'It's very thoughtful and sweet of you, but I'd better go back if you don't mind, Carey. I've had a wonderful day thanks to you and it's been marvellous seeing you again,' she added hastily.

'It's been great for me also.' The voice was level and held no displeasure. His face had moved nearer. 'You'll take care on these toy town roads?'

'I will.' He hadn't made a definite date to see her again. She wasn't conscious of turning her head fully towards him, but suddenly her mouth was covered by his, her lips falling apart under the growing pressure. Just seconds. Then his voice was away from her — a million miles away.

'Goodnight, Stella.'

She struggled to attain normality again. Fumbled with the door. 'G — goodnight, Carey.' Her throat was dry, her breath catching. Moments later she sank unsteadily into the cold, small interior of her own car. Alongside she heard Carey's throb into life and in a few moments its tail lights were growing smaller, to be lost to sight round the bend in the road.

4

Stella's thoughts were chaotic as she drove home. Had she thrown away her chance of seeing him? Probably he would never get in touch with her again. In any case he did not have her address as she had not given it to him, nor did she remember him asking for it. He had no doubt had enough of her. His suggestions that she should stay overnight at the hotel had been well meant so that she would not have to be on the road at night. And yet all she had thought of was that he might attempt to seduce her. No doubt he had guessed her thoughts and would even now be laughing at her prudishness and naïvety. She wanted him so badly yet she had shied away at his suggestion that they spend the night under the same roof. He would regard the time spent together that day as a pleasant interlude

— no more than that. His kiss in the car had been a kiss of goodbye. Fate had given her a second chance and she had refused to take it.

Three weeks later a letter arrived for her from Carey. The paper trembled in her hands as she read it just before setting off to the school. Would she come to Foxholme the following weekend, Saturday morning or early afternoon? By the tone of the letter she was expected to come. Her heart sang. So the last kiss had not been a goodbye one after all. Fate was giving her another chance and this was sure to be the last. But she was puzzled as to how he had obtained her address.

About one o'clock on Saturday found her on the road out of Windermere. It was a calm hazy day with a prospect of a very warm afternoon to come. She glanced at the overnight bag on the seat beside her. Just in case he did ask her to stay this time she had come prepared. She had decided to drive up in her own car, feeling more independent by doing so.

Stella swung the car in between the pillars at the entrance to the driveway. She saw the gold coloured letters 'Foxholme' inset into the stonework. She drove slowly up the gently curving driveway. There was a glimpse of a building, hydrangeas, daffodils and short conifer bushes to her left, tall trees to her right. Then the drive began to widen, the car wheels crunching over the rose coloured surface on to a large oblong frontage before the house. Three other cars were parked there. Stella recognised Carey's Rolls convertible.

Stella made a conscious effort to release her tightened grip on the steering wheel as she brought her own humble saloon to a halt. A fever held her. Was she building up, reading too much into her friendship with Carey? She glanced at the house, stone built and solid with a warm colouring to it, with ivy etching the trailing greenery across it. A glass-fronted conservatory, or possibly what had been a stable, adjoined the right hand side of the house. Something glinted from inside. Above balconies caught her eyes. A house she guessed that concealed its size by its discreet architecture.

For a moment she stood facing the house hesitating, then the tops of sun umbrellas caught her eye beyond the cars. A few people were sat on a patio in front of open french windows. One detached himself from the group and came towards her. It was Carey, dark-trousered, with a white chest-hugging shirt and hand outstretched to take hers.

'Welcome, Stella, great to see you again. Have any difficulty finding Foxholme?'

Stirring herself out of the trance-like state her mind went into when in his presence, she replied, 'Your directions were first class, Carey; they helped enormously,' and wondered if she sounded like a school-teacher. Nodding at the building she said, 'Have you settled in all right?' She felt the floodlamps turned on again when he regarded her.

'It's been easy to do that, Stella, and I'll give you a guided tour later.' He gestured in the direction of the other people on the patio. 'We're just having cocktails. Come and join us.'

She hesitated looking down to give a fleeting appraisal of herself, somewhat dusty and travel stained.

Carey must have observed it. 'You look well, Stella, take my word.'

She was happy to, and, confidence restored, allowed him to take her towards the group, one hand still holding hers, the other resting reassuringly across her waist.

'My guest from Yorkshire,' announced Carey, 'Miss Stella Bardon. We met on an island in the middle of the ocean. She popped up just when I thought the island was all mine.' He turned to the couple nearest to him, the man wiry and of about fifty with a grey full head of hair and bright blue eyes. 'Meet Harold Bilby. I have Harold to thank for Foxholme. He very kindly sold it to me.'

'He wanted it so badly we had to get

out,' smiled Harold.

'And this is Amanda, his daughter,' said Carey. Stella remembered then where she had seen them before. They were the couple who had met Carey near the jetty at Ambleside when she had made rather a fool of herself. Amanda Bilby was beautiful in a dark striking way, immaculately groomed and coiffured and dressed in maroon. The dark stare held an animosity for an instant, then the face was blandly smiling its owner's greeting and letting the eyes slide over Stella in a carelessly insolent manner.

Stella, in a trouser suit of off-white with a green and white hooped top below it, began to feel that perhaps she should have worn something dressier. She was glad to turn and be introduced to the others.

Carey then fetched her a vodka and pineapple and Stella chatted easily with everyone except Amanda. She was conscious of Amanda staring at her and was acutely aware also of the fact that

that person must have witnessed Stella's discomfiture when Carey had walked straight past her without recognising her at Ambleside. Stella's face burned at the memory.

Carey raised his glass. 'To a fine weekend,' at which there was a chorus of agreement. The sentiment was echoed in Stella's heart. To a fine weekend certainly, but not so much regarding the weather as to the time spent near her host which couldn't be anything else but fine, beautiful and exciting. Then her Yorkshire common sense made her wonder if her romance had gone as far as it could. Would she, after this weekend, be remembered only as another overnight guest?

She sipped at her drink thinking what a lovely setting it was with the haze beginning to disappear and the sun warming and yellowing everything. Just over the tops of the trees beyond the terracing and lawn she glimpsed the sparkle of the lake.

She became aware of Carey leaning

over her. 'Whenever you want to unpack, your room's ready Stella.'

Carey waited until she retrieved her bag from the car then took it from her. He looked at her provocatively — a teasing light in his eyes.

'I'm glad you brought it with you. I wouldn't have taken no for an answer this time.'

Behind the easy words and banter she saw and heard a desire in him that made her breathless.

Carey led her to the wide staircase leading from the hall. At its foot he turned to her. 'That's a very nice outfit you're wearing, Stella — it looks fabulous on you.' Things were improving, she thought. When she had arrived he had said she looked well. She smiled with pleasure at him and murmured something about it being suitable for the Lake District.

Just at that moment a door opened just off the hall and an elderly woman appeared. Carey stopped and motioned the woman over. 'Stella, I want you to meet a very important person in my new house. This is Florence my housekeeper and cook. I'm very lucky — she came with the house and I think she's taken me over with it.'

The buxom figure faced Stella, the blue eyes in the still fresh complexion set in a round face, and the grey hair in an old fashioned bun. 'Pleased to meet you, Miss Stella.' With a longer skirt, a white apron around her front and an old fashioned servant's cap she could have come straight out of an earlier century.

Carey chuckled as he glanced from Stella to Florence. 'Florence is a chef, but she won't allow me to call her that — she thinks that it sounds too important.' His eyes sparkled mischievously. 'But I think you'll agree with me Stella when you've sampled her cooking that she deserves something better than cook.' He turned again towards the stairs and the stout figure hustled off, obviously pleased at her employer's praise.

At the top Stella accompanied Carey along an open-railed gallery from which she could see down into the hall. Carey stopped at a door on the far side opposite the stairs and opened it for her, putting her bag just inside.

'Your room, Stella, hope you like it. There's no hurry. Lunch will be ready when you are.' His look lingered on her as he shut the door slowly behind him, but not before Stella with some surprise glimpsed the girl Amanda looking up from the hall below. Stella was secretly pleased — she had felt her disapproval of her as soon as they had met. Amanda had not wanted her at Foxholme. Stella shrugged, it was just too bad, she turned back into the room.

It was a beautiful room with a modern four poster bed with a canopy in pale green velvet. Beyond it were open glass doors to a balcony. Voices floated up from below. The lake lay blue-silver beyond the trees and toy-like boats appeared to be motionless upon it.

Stella then luxuriated in a hot bath thinking what a vastly different world to her own she had joined for the weekend. As she had realised previously her host was obviously a very successful man. And yet how often since she had become reacquainted with him had she seen the swift shadows of some inner conflict come and go. The other guests were very pleasant apart from Amanda who definitely had plans for Carey mused Stella, but then so had she herself. Amanda was beautiful, though; everything about her seemed to be right, and she was obviously used to the good things of life. Nothing it seemed had put wrinkles on her brow. Stella sighed. Was she out of her depth? She guessed Amanda thought so.

As she dressed Stella cheered herself with the thought that she had met Carey before Amanda — had known him longer.

When she was ready to go downstairs Stella took a final look at herself in the mirror. She saw dark blue flared trousers, a blue and white hooped top and white shoes, a white jacket slung over her shoulder, fair hair encircled with a matching blue polka dot bandana. The face below was flushed and not just from her bath. Play it cool she told herself. The eyes staring back at her were as open as a shop window, frank and revealing.

Lunch was marvellous and Stella remarked that it must have been hard work for Florence but then learned from Carey that she had further help in the kitchen for the weekend guests.

'Did you think that I am a tyrant to my household?' Carey surveyed her with some amusement.

'No, of course not.' She knew Amanda was gazing at her with an annoying condescending curling of the lips, and Stella began to wish she hadn't spoken. 'It was just that I couldn't imagine her coping with all this — she's not young.' She felt awkward, and must appear gauche.

Carey put up a hand in mock horror.

'Please don't let her hear you say that. I may lose one of the best in the business.'

He continued to regard her teasingly. 'You've just given me one great idea. Why don't you come and take over the household and that will leave Florence free to apply her kitchen skills?'

Oh why did he have to be so cruel? She would have left her job and jumped at the chance just to be near him. Aloud her answer was laboured through her smile. 'Well I suppose it would be a change from looking after children all day.' Stella noticed that Amanda's eyes had narrowed in her expression of studied indifference. Obviously she didn't care for the invitation to Stella, even if it was not intended to be taken seriously.

'Then perhaps I'll make an offer the school cannot refuse to let you go.' An electrical charge seemed to radiate from him holding her prisoner until he chose to look away at Amanda. 'It's no use me asking Amanda. She's used to the bright lights of modelling.'

'I'll give it a thought, Carey, sounds interesting,' said Amanda easily, her fingers splayed out and slipping slowly down his forearm. All the same Stella sensed her unease as Amanda shot a glance across the table at her.

After lunch Stella and the others sat outside for coffee on the terrace, the afternoon being warm with a few white clouds dancing on the hill tops across the lake.

Later Carey took them to see the collection of cars he had acquired. They were housed in the glass-fronted building at the side of the house that Stella had noticed on her arrival. They were all from an earlier era of motoring, each one a convertible, sleek and beautiful and at rest. Stella realised that she was forgotten for the moment in his obvious enthusiasm over the cars, and she noticed Amanda had remained on the terrace, bored and petulant mouthed.

Afterwards some of the guests went to the tennis courts others sauntered along the lawns. Stella watched from the patio. How lovely everything was. The sounds of ball on racket came, and voices. She had an idea that Carey was playing and no doubt Amanda would be with him. Suddenly she didn't feel too happy.

Wandering slowly along the front of the house Stella paused by the open door of the garage housing the collection of cars. She stepped just inside eyeing a pink and maroon roadster. She went up to it and touched it, letting her hand rest along the top of its door. She thought about the people who might have owned it in those far off days. How many glamorous women had ridden in it? Stella pictured them making an arrival at theatres, flapper balls, county parties — the rich — the famous. Perhaps a film star had owned it. She dreamed on, the crowd, the cameras, the applause.

'You go well together — an elegant matching pair.' The voice startled Stella and she turned quickly. Carey stood in the doorway surveying her. He came towards her slowly.

'I didn't mean to startle you. I just wondered where you were. Now I find you in here all by yourself.' His gaze searched her face enquiringly.

Stella laughed shortly, a trifle uncomfortable that he should find her in there alone. He must think she was an odd ball person. 'Oh I was just strolling about, came in to have another look.' She gestured at the cars. 'I can understand you being enthusiastic over them.'

He gave a shrug of his strong shoulders. 'Oh, sure, they're beautiful, but they're only metal. They can't give me real happiness — only a substitute.' There was a longing in his tone. He seemed to be increasing in size, filling the space above her. His voice descended to a whispering caress. 'But you're beautiful and alive, Stella.' Somehow he was very close without her having seen him move. The words were wonderful to hear, and it was unbelievable that he should be saying them to her. His warm hands rested on her shoulders, then drew her to him. His lips sealed hers. Weakly she moulded against him, the world telescoped to just his mouth.

The touch of paradise was ended almost as soon as it had begun, the door to the museum closing with a bang. Carey let her go, turning quickly. Past him Stella thought she glimpsed the back of Amanda disappearing round the corner of the building, tennis racket in hand.

The spell broken, Stella stepped away, but still bemused by the incident and Carey looked at her with dulled eyes from which desire had not yet receded fully. 'My fault,' he said huskily. 'I told her that I was coming up for a drink.' A wry smile touched his face. 'Which I was.' He sighed, 'But I guess it turned out differently, life has a habit of doing that.' His smile expanded rue-fully. 'Well, I've lost my tennis partner it seems,' and extended his hand to her. 'Would you care to partner me?'

Partner him! She certainly would, for life preferably, but for the time being she must make the most of his offer.

They played gentle tennis for about twenty minutes, he a real athlete, balanced and easy-moving. She gained the impression that he was more interested in observing her than playing the game. She wasn't a good player, but she didn't care. Her heart was singing, her feet moving just above the ground, and the trees round the court nodding as if giving their approval of the man in whose arms she had been not so long before.

5

That evening after dinner Carey surprised her by informing the others present of her entry for the cross lake swim in a few weeks' time. Stella was sure they wouldn't want to hear about it, but she was further surprised at the interest shown.

'What I'd like to do is to sponsor Stella for any deserving charity she names. I'm sure she has one. It will give me an opportunity to show my gratitude for the kindness I've received as an American here in England. If anyone wants to join me they're welcome.'

Everybody thought it was a good idea apart from Amanda who nodded but didn't say anything.

'You're looking very serious, Stella. D'you mind if we sponsor you?'

'No, not at all, it's very generous of

you, Carey, and thanks everybody.' She laughed half seriously. 'I wouldn't dare fail now. I shall just have to get across that lake.'

'I guess that's settled then,' said Carey. 'All that you've got to do now is tell us which charity or organisation you want the proceeds to go to.'

Stella didn't really have to think about which charity she would choose. Her own and her sister's background came immediately into her mind. She nodded firmly, spoke enthusiastically. 'Yes, I certainly do have one — the society for orphans and adoption of children' — in her own class she had a few adopted children.

'That's a great idea, Stella. You can give me the address and details later.' For a moment his eyes lingered on her, the warmth from them washing over her and titillating her senses once more.

After dinner music for dancing was played by a trio in another room overlooking the lawn. Once Carey took her into his arms and held her close as they danced. She breathed her thanks for his sponsorship of her coming swim. 'I hope I don't let you down.'

'You won't,' he smiled down at her. 'Just think of all those orphans — that will keep you going.' He paused then went on, 'But I want you to do something for me tomorrow.'

'If I can of course,' she murmured wonderingly.

'Well, in the morning I want you to go along to the garage where the old cars are.' A glint of humour showed in his eyes. 'Alone. I want you to take a good long look at each car, and then I want you to choose the one you like the best. O.K.?'

She nodded mystified.

'Right, when you've picked it let me know and I'll donate that car to your adoption society or auction it and they'll get the money.'

Stella stopped dancing and stared up at him astounded. 'You — you can't do that,' she stammered.

A frown touched his face. 'Honey,

they're mine, I can.'

She struggled with her thoughts. 'I mean — they're too valuable to give away.'

'One,' he corrected.

'Well, all right, but you've collected them.'

'Isn't this adoption and orphan organisation a valuable thing to you?'

'Oh, yes,' she affirmed strongly.

'And don't they always need as much money as they can get?'

Stella remembered the flag days, and the fund raising efforts by some of the societies. But this was different — he was going to give away a valuable and historic car. It was an overwhelmingly generous offer.

'You'll do it?' He guided her back to a chair. She nodded still not quite able to come to terms with what he had proposed.

She did not get a chance to talk to him alone again until much later, he spending the intervening time chatting and having the occasional dance

— once with Amanda. It was when she saw people drifting off to bed that Stella realised just how tired she herself was. Carey was nowhere to be seen so she made her way upstairs.

Just as she approached her bedroom she heard a door behind her opening, and looking over her shoulder she saw Carey.

He came towards her slowly, his gaze roving over her. 'Leaving us so soon, Stella?'

'I saw some of the others going up, then I realised that I felt tired myself.'

'Maybe it was the tennis this afternoon.'

More likely, she guessed, that it was the tension from being in love with him. Had their kiss in the garage meant anything to him? Take an embrace where you could, was that his creed? His eyes were smiling into hers now. Was it with a veiled mockery? Did he now believe that she was a simple shallow girl going to bed early and interested only in swimming?

'Get a good night's sleep then, Stella.'

Carey half turned away then looked back at her. 'If the weather's fine I thought about a day on the lake tomorrow. How would you like to make the acquaintance of *Fair Wind* again?'

Anything to be near him. 'I'd like that very much Carey.'

Carey hesitated fractionally. 'Until the morning then. Goodnight.'

She spoke after him. 'And thanks for the sponsoring offer — it really was kind of you.'

He came back to stand in front of her, and closer than he had been before. 'It will give me great pleasure, Stella, and so will this.' She was quite unprepared for the spread of his hands on her upper arms and the brushing of his lips against hers. Then he was walking away along the gallery before she opened her eyes.

After a late breakfast the weekend party took off down to the lake to board *Fair Wind* and there a surprise awaited them. Kindon Ferrers the English actor famous for his detective series joined them. It appeared that he was an old friend of Carey's and had accepted the latter's invitation and had flown up to be with them for the remainder of the weekend.

This time Carey headed *Fair Wind* for the southern end of Windermere. The day was lovely but with a stronger breeze and just right for sailing. The lake became narrow towards the southern shore with the sombre hills around rising as if from sleep to warm themselves. And behind them the rearing twin heads of the mountainous Langdale Pikes.

Stella gazed out over the lovely scene, but then a fleeting sadness came over her. How Pauline, her sister, would have enjoyed a day out such as this. But she had seemed happy enough in her latest letter.

'I don't want to interrupt any secret thoughts, but what would you like to drink?' Carey's voice stroked her.

Quickly she returned into the present to meet his gaze which held a slight concern. 'Anything wrong? Something I've said, can't be anything I've done.' His eyes carried the implication with a flickering amusement.

'No, no — just admiring the view,' she smiled. It was after all a minor worry.

She watched him as he went to fetch her drink; the view was good on board too. He was wearing a white tee shirt and shorts, sandals on his feet, the white peaked cap shielding his eyes.

Along the deck she could see Amanda sporting herself half reclining on an air bed and talking to Kindon Ferrers. At least, thought Stella, he was keeping her away from Carey.

Carey returned with her glass then glanced at Stella's headwear. 'I like the hat, honey, it suits you — you look nautical as well as pretty.'

Stella was glad of the compliment, having wondered whether the small sailor type hat she sported looked rather ridiculous. It was her attempt to add something to the fashion scene aboard the yacht.

Carey anchored *Fair Wind* right at the southern end of the lake. Then champagne and food were consumed and guests found comfortable positions for themselves. Stella was sat in the cockpit when Kindon joined her. They chatted and she was treated to an up to date account of his recent locations and his new series in particular. He was a charming quick-talking companion, full of a restless nervous energy. After he had refilled Stella's glass with champagne he said, 'I've heard all about this meeting of yours with Carey on that island.'

'Oh, he's told you all about it has he?' Stella remarked ruefully. 'I suppose I was an idiot, but I just don't know how I came to miss that boat back to the ship.'

Kindon laughed sympathetically, then his face became unexpectedly serious as he went on, 'I'm glad you did miss the boat.'

Stella gazed at him with surprise.

'Oh, why? How d'you mean?'

Kindon Ferrers frowned reflectively. 'Well the last time I saw Carey was in New York — I was doing a play on Broadway at the time. I came across him and he seemed really down and out.' Kindon put up a hand at Stella's raised eyebrows and shook his head shortly. 'Oh, no, not financially, I don't mean that way, not Carey. No, er — he looked haunted and frankly I was disturbed at the way he'd changed, and don't forget we'd known each other for a long number of years.' He paused and Stella waited impatiently with an anxious intensity.

'It wasn't physical, he looked all right in that respect, but something was eating him mentally.'

Stella remembered the pain that had been noticeable in his eyes on occasions.

'Did you ever find out the cause?' she asked.

Kindon waved a hand. 'Oh, I gathered it was over some woman. He didn't say much about it, but don't get me wrong though, they ran after him.' Her companion smiled wistfully. 'Some guys have all the luck Stella.'

Stella was keen to hear more about Carey's background. 'Was it a break up?'

Kindon frowned deeply, thoughtfully. 'No-o, I don't think so. It was different this time.'

'This time?' A quick hurt pricked her and she began to wish she had not been so inquisitive.

Kindon studied her knowingly. 'He's human, Stella, you must realise. Up to a few years ago women came and went in his life. But I think he's changed, we all do.'

'And this woman — did she change him?' If she was going to delve into Carey's life, she would have to steel herself — she couldn't alter what had happened before she met him.

'It's possible, he was certainly cut up about her. Funny thing is I don't think he loved her in the slightest. In fact I once heard him say he'd be glad when she died.'

Stella was shocked — he must have hated her. Seeing Carey as he was that day it was difficult to imagine him having such fierce and intense ill-feeling towards a woman as to want to see her dead. 'And where is this woman now?' In a way she must have been something special thought Stella.

Kindon gave her a strange look and hesitated before answering. 'I've no idea.' The actor shrugged. 'He just said she'd gone out of his life, and that's all I got out of him the last time.' Kindon glanced over his shoulder at Carey, busy conversing with other guests, then spoke with great conviction. 'I know this, he's a darn sight happier than I've seen him in years. Maybe it's got something to do with you, Stella,' he suggested with a grin.

She prayed that it had. 'But I haven't seen him very often.'

'Once is sometimes enough,' Kindon commented. He looked at her keenly.

'You like him, don't you, Stella?'

Like him! That was the understatement of all time. She nodded. 'I'm afraid I do.' She was also afraid of the hurt and heartbreak that could be hers if she persisted with the relationship.

'I wish you all the luck in the world. You're probably just the girl he needs.'

'But don't you ever feel like settling down sometime, Kindon?'

Kindon shook his head. 'Well, you know how it is, it wouldn't be fair to any woman. I've too many commitments, I'm here and there. How many stay together in our profession?'

How lucky people were, like Kindon, she thought, being married to their profession, and leaving their heart to take care of itself. That way they didn't get hurt.

The object of her musing spoke again. 'Carey mentioned the swim of yours that's coming up. I'd like to come and support you — moral support if not physical.'

'It's very kind of you, thanks

Kindon.' How very flattering to have a handsome wealthy man to invite you to his house party, and then to meet a star of stage and screen.

Carey came down the steps from the deck into the cockpit and stood over them. 'See what happens when I turn my back,' he said in mock annoyance. 'I saw her first, Kindon.' He looked down at Stella. 'You've got to be wary of these film types — they move fast.'

Kindon rose. 'Well you shouldn't leave a pretty girl like this unattended. She was all by herself and looking rather wistful.' He sighed. 'I'll leave you two together, then.' With a wave he left them to join the others.

Carey sat down close concentrating his attention on Stella. The effect on her was like being wrapped in a warm cloud. 'I'm sorry if you were left by yourself. I was busy . . . '

'I was quite happy,' she broke in. He would think that she was a little girl who couldn't be left for a moment.

Carey's gaze missed nothing. 'Are

you enjoying yourself Stella?'

'Yes I am, Carey,' she replied definitely. 'It's fabulous.' She felt some regret. In a few hours she would be going home again. The dream would be over.

'The pleasure is all mine Stella Bardon.' She smiled at his use of both her names, her senses lulled and soothed by his softly murmured words. They came again, his hands caressing hers. 'You will stay overnight? I want you to and I will not take no for an answer this time.' His delivery was gentle but there was no denying the determination in his expression.

She did not reply at once, hearing the slap of water against the sides of *Fair Wind*. He must be aware of the pounding gong which was her heart. An opportunity to be with him a while longer. She could leave early on Monday and drive like the devil. It wasn't like her to take extra time off apart from her holidays, but this was her life and this man who was asking her to stay overnight was also part of her life — at least she wanted him to be — an inseparable part of it.

She allowed herself to be captured by his eyes again. 'All right Carey, if you insist.' Her voice was dry sounding.

'I do.' He took her hand. 'Now come along, I can't have you languishing by yourself again. I'm going to share you with the others.'

Carey was as excellent an on-board host as he was off it, perhaps too good because she did not get a chance to speak alone with him again until much later.

It was a languid memorable afternoon, Carey moving *Fair Wind* from one delectable spot to another. Some went swimming over the side, whilst the occasional water skier flashed by. The steady passage of steamers packed with people and the northern frame of mountains in the distance. This was another world thought Stella and how ordinary her life would seem when she was back at work.

6

About six o'clock Carey berthed *Fair Wind* and the party then went back to Foxholme to change ready for dinner later. The evening passed by pleasantly for Stella with the added thrill running through her that Carey wanted to talk to her alone. Had he not asked her specially to spend another night at Foxholme? But by eleven o'clock he had not made any attempt to seek her out. She was disappointed but excused him with the thought that being the host he had not had much time to spend with her. Stella noticed that Amanda made herself very available at Carey's side. Afterwards there was dancing and Stella danced once with Kindon — she liked him. In fact if there had never been a Carey Ganton the evening would have been marvellous enough in the actor's company.

At nearly midnight and with a growing let down feeling, she decided to turn in. Catching Carey's eye she waved and mouthed a goodnight. He glanced sideways, smiling easily at her, half raised a hand and then turned back to his guests.

In bed she stared into the darkness of the canopy above, thinking that it had hardly been worth staying on another night and that she should have gone home earlier. It now appeared that all he had wanted was the satisfaction of getting her to say that she would stay overnight. And Amanda, she could afford to be patient and would have ample time and opportunity to see him.

Despondently her thoughts ran on. In the morning she would thank him politely and drive away. She had had a good weekend and it must be regarded as just an interlude in her life. With a dismal sigh she turned on her side, the half drawn curtains of the four poster now making the night oppressive.

A knock came on her door, startling

her. Before she could answer it opened slightly, the subdued light from the gallery striping the bedroom floor. A voice came — Carey's — in a deep whisper. 'Are you awake Stella? May I talk to you for a moment?'

Was she awake! His very presence charged her body with a pulsating life. In seconds she was sat up and calling softly — a breathless eager sound — for him to enter. Pulling the curtain aside she saw his dim figure slip into the room.

'I was undecided about coming, but couldn't get the chance earlier.'

'It's all right Carey, I've only just turned in.' She tried to sound matter of fact, but found it very difficult with her heart fluttering madly. The trouble was when she was near this man her body wanted to take over, her mind trailing in second place.

'I wanted to tell you,' Carey said, 'that I'm going back to the States this next week.'

'Oh!' In the stillness of the room her

jerky utterance revealed utter surprise and disappointment. Was he going out of her life again?

Carey interpreted the sound correctly. 'I'll be back — I'm not going to give up all this now that I've just settled in.'

Relief flooded Stella's being, but did 'all this' include her?

Stella was aware that he had moved a step toward the bed. 'I'll leave you my address now and phone number as I may not get the opportunity in the morning. You said you were leaving early.'

'I must,' she murmured regretfully. Stretching out her arm she switched the bedside lamp on, its circle of light bathing her side of the bed and revealing Carey, his shirt unbuttoned almost to his waist. It was as if he had been preparing for bed and then had decided to visit her.

He produced a pen, leaned forward. 'Have you anything I can write on?'

There was a notebook in her bag she

knew. Her hand was unsteady as she lifted it over on to the bed and her breathing had shortened. She watched as he wrote, observing the dark head bent over in concentration. She wanted to reach out and pull it down to her.

'There,' he said, dotting the page firmly, 'you will have it just in case.'

In case of what? Or had he just wanted an excuse to enter her bedroom — and bed. His speech had become husky she realised.

Her fingers grasped one end of the notebook as he handed it back to her. An inch apart from his at the other end. Too late, he had let go. What did the name and address matter when he was there just two feet away from her? Dropping the notebook into her bag again she slid the latter on to the bedside table.

He continued to stand there, a feverish light in his regard of her. 'There's something I've got to ask of you. You're leaving here tomorrow, and before I go to America I must know — I must.' He

110

spoke with an effort from a long way down, strained and throaty, and suddenly apparently unsure of himself, so strange in a man such as he.

Her own voice sounded like that of a stranger when it came. 'If — if I can help. W — what is it?'

'For the first time in my life I've fallen in love, Stella — with you — and — and what I must know is, will you marry me?'

She raised her eyes swiftly at the shock of those beautiful words, her feelings for him expressed so clearly in them, and her sigh contained delirious excitement and acceptance.

Tenderly at first, his mouth moved on hers with ever increasing and savage pressure until her lips submitted helplessly beneath his.

Fire rose and spread lightning fast through her veins, having smouldered from the spark he had kindled the day before during their kiss in the garage. A tiny impotent voice of warning sounded. Had she fallen for the oldest trick in the business? But then her mind faded to nothing under this total assault on her senses. The curtains of the four poster seemed to be bending in and over her and its top fading into the darkness above . . .

The light of Monday morning brought her awake. Surely it had been a dream — he had asked her to marry him! She had accepted. Half turning she put out a hand tentatively and moved it over the space beside her. There was no-one else, she was alone in the bed. As her brain cleared she knew that Carey had shared it. They had made love, rampantly, passionately. He had said he loved her. Where was he now? Perhaps he had left her early to avoid the risk of the other guests finding out that they had slept together.

She stretched and glanced out of the window. But it didn't matter what the day was like now. Her heart was joyous and full of the man in whose arms she had lain last night. A Monday morning like no other she had known. Faint qualms presented themselves. She had given herself to Carey, but it had been in love. Was that the end, just another conquest for him? She looked at herself in the mirror. Tumble-haired, but below it the face was radiant and love stared out of the blue eyes.

Brushing her hair back she dismissed those thoughts immediately. Another intruded — a very mundane one — work. She must hurry.

Her watch was on the bedside table where she had put it last night. Another one lay next to it. It was Carey's; he must have forgotten it. She had noticed it before, resting on the dark springy hairs of his wrist. Putting it to her breast she guessed that her heart was beating faster than the watch. It conjured up again his powerful body making her a willing prisoner in the darkness of the night before.

With an effort she broke off from her fantasising and noted the time. Oh! if only she did not have to return to work.

Hers had been an all too brief sojourn in heaven.

She replaced Carey's watch on the bedside table. As she turned away her fingers caught the end of the projecting strap, knocking the watch to the floor. Anxiously she bent to retrieve it, seeing with relief that the second hand was still moving. It was then that she saw that the back had sprung open. Just as she was about to close it she glimpsed colour. Curious she opened the casing of the watch wider. Inside was a photograph fitting neatly against the metal. A dark haired woman's face stared up at her — a stranger. She then noticed an inscription on the inner half of the casing. It read 'To Carey on our wedding day, Estelle'.

The shock paralysed her brain for long seconds as if it had fused, and she groped to understand. The face was still there together with the words. One fact, bludgeoning through the numbness pervading her. He was married! Carey was married!

The watch fell from her fingers as if it were a poisonous snake, and she slipped to her knees down the side of the bed in utter misery, heartbreak and sorrow mixed in her tears, wetting the bed cover over which Carey had leaned when asking her to marry him. The same cover which had cocooned them as she had lain in his arms that night.

But then an anger was born from her tears. Carey was just a cheap jack, married, and had slept with her and had been wearing the watch with his wife's photograph in it when he had proposed marriage just a few hours ago. He had used his charm on her — a shark on the lookout for a victim, and she had been a wide-eyed romantic fool. Oh, how easy it had been for him. He had promised her marriage. It was all so clear now. Being married certainly hadn't stopped him from making a play for her. She squirmed inside herself at the wanton way she had given herself to him that night. How Carey must be congratulating himself. Stella felt sick and cold, but at the same time her face burned with shame. An expensive yacht and a handsome face had turned her head so easily. Her mind was in a torment from the shattering knowledge just gained. Had Carey forgotten that the photograph was in the watch or had he ever cared? No doubt he had been so confident of his power over her, but it didn't matter now.

Savagely she threw her clothes into her case. She hated him now, also the house and couldn't get away from the place quickly enough. It was well named for its owner. Foxholme — a fox, cunning and lying in wait for its prey. Her love star had disintegrated into a common dust. Amanda would be next — she could have him with pleasure.

With a sob rising in her throat she flung the door open — to find Carey coming up the stairs.

He looked at her in utter surprise. 'Stella! You're not leaving so soon? We've such a lot to talk about and arrange, my love. I want to announce our . . . '

Her ragged torn emotions erupted again. 'You're a crook, a conman — you should be behind bars where you cannot hurt anyone else. The only thing I want you to announce is that I'm leaving now,' she threw at him fiercely, broken-voiced.

Sheer shocked amazement showed on the face opposite. The warmth and unrestrained delight that had been evident on his seeing her drained away. 'I — what do you mean, what's wrong Stella?' He moved towards her, hands outstretched. 'Just tell me.'

She stepped backwards quickly. 'Don't touch me,' she croaked. 'You've done all the touching you're going to do. Try Amanda, I'm sure you'll be just as successful.' Dropping her case Stella dashed back into the bedroom and grabbed the watch off the floor. Thrust it into his hands, the photograph uppermost. 'Your wife,' she flung at him, her eyes flashing, her anger lightning blue.

The pain and hurt was bared in his eyes and it gave her a vicarious pleasure as she brushed past him. 'Wait!' The sound was torn from him, but she ignored it. 'You don't understand, Stella, please.'

Tears made the stairs misty as she stumbled downwards. 'Oh, yes I do — you're contemptible,' she shouted over her shoulder. Faces stared at her in the hall.

Flinging herself into the car she drove quickly down to the gates, catching a glimpse of her distraught face in the mirror. This couldn't be her, dashing away from the man she thought she loved above all else until half an hour before. Surely it must be a bad dream — the cliché she'd read in countless romances.

Stella drove home automatically. A lovely morning with the early summer greenery unfolding in old lakeland. For her it was Monday morning, and a black Monday at that — one that engulfed her heart in a hopeless misery.

Once home she collapsed, weary and exhausted mentally. Later she recovered enough to phone her school and make some excuse about being down with a virus. Her lips, bruised from Carey's kisses the night before, twisted bitterly. Her excuse wasn't far from the truth. A virus had invaded her — a love virus. And the sooner she got rid of the memories it carried, the better for her.

7

The following weeks were terrible for her as she strove to get some order and balance into her life again. A letter arrived during that first week, bearing the Windermere postmark. She tore it open and on seeing Carey's signature tore it up without reading a single word.

Later when she could think about the affair with a degree of calmness she marvelled at how she had come to meet Carey on that island. Sometimes she thought about the watch and the photograph that had lain in it. He had kept the photograph there which puzzled her. It did not seem like the action of a man who had had no feeling for the person who had given it to him. On the other hand it was more likely that he had just forgotten about her and it. And yet she could not forget the hurt in his eyes when she had thrust the watch into his hand that morning. Then Stella's mind would start to spin and for her own sanity she had to stop thinking about the affair.

About a month after that disastrous weekend at Foxholme a different kind of letter arrived, from the lake swim association, confirming her entry for the event. Her first thought was that she would not go but would cancel her entry. She felt that she did not want to see or hear of anything to do with Windermere again. It held too many painful memories which were easily aroused. And yet why should she let that single unfortunate incident dictate against something she normally enjoyed? Was her life henceforth going to be governed by memories of what could have been?

Would Carey be there? She doubted it. All that talk about sponsorship had been for her benefit, a come up and see my etchings — a new angle. But supposing he was there? She would ignore him and get on with the swim. She sighed. It had been a bitter lesson, but next time, if there was to be another one, she would defend her heart more stoutly.

She glanced at the rules governing the swim. Six p.m. prompt at Ambleside with two crew members in the escort boat, who were to row her over for the start at the other side of the lake, but also to get her back into the boat in case she got into difficulties during the swim. Stella was glad that the notification had come, as it would help to keep her mind and body occupied for the next few weeks.

Three o'clock on the day of the swim found Stella on the road to Windermere. From past experience she knew that it was a mistake to arrive too early, as hanging around waiting did not do any good. However tensions of a different sort began to assail her as she approached Windermere. Just supposing she saw Carey, and if he should speak to her. Her insides twisted at the thought, she feeling that she would not be able to acknowledge him or even bear having him near her. She assured herself that there wasn't much chance that he would be there. Nevertheless she couldn't prevent herself from glancing at his house as she drove past.

On arrival Stella was surprised to find how busy the area around the beach and car park was. She couldn't remember the swim attracting so many on-lookers before. Sometimes when the weather had been poor there had only been a handful present, and those usually looking on with pity as the competitors staggered ashore.

Stella changed in the car, then waited until she saw her crew arrive before getting out. Then with her companions she broke the fringe of onlookers, pulling her track suit hood well over her face and trying to look as inconspicuous as possible. She made for the small group of competitors gathered near the water's edge and collected the card with her number on. Number six. There would be prizes for the first ones across, and for the others certificates of completion marked with the time taken.

The rowing boats were lined up ready for the swimmers and their crews to embark. The water was calm, the evening fine and the sun poised above the hills to her right. It should be a good crossing. There had been times in the past when the lake had looked like a miniature sea.

In a few minutes they were clear of the beach and heading on a diagonal course for the far side of the lake. She did not look back, being only too well aware of the increasing distance between herself and what would be the finish in about an hour's time. Stella sat in the stern as her crew pulled on the oars. Her own hard work would commence soon. Glancing about her she saw the other boats strung out across the lake and tried not to think about how deep it was at that point.

Something blue caught her eye in the

distance immediately to her right. A blue-hulled yacht. Why hadn't she noticed it before? It was almost certainly the yacht *Fair Wind*. Stella turned away regretting fiercely that it had attracted her attention.

She hunched into her track suit reflecting bitterly on the time when her heart turned over with joy and anticipation on seeing the yacht. How things had changed. Was he on board? Had he come to gloat over his latest conquest? Even at that moment he might have his binoculars trained on her — searching her expression. Well she wouldn't give him the satisfaction of letting him see that the sight of the craft had affected her.

They were nearing the starting point, and some of the swimmers whose boats had already arrived were peeling off track suits and adjusting goggles. Stella felt her boat touch bottom and come to rest. This was it! She took off her track suit to reveal her blue and white one-piece costume, then pushed her hair under a white cap, and shivered slightly at the touch of the evening breeze on her skin.

The boats now began to move offshore to await their particular swimmer when the race began. Good luck wishes came from her crew. Tensely she smiled, 'See you over there,' and stepped into the water.

The cold made her gasp as she waded into deeper water up to her waist. She edged into position with the others. Beyond the line of swimmers she saw the official launch with starter and doctor on board. The starter was waving an arm for someone to get back. Oh damn! Did a few inches matter? Stella gazed into the distance at the tiny looking buildings so far away where the swim would finish. It was always the same in those last few seconds. What the hell was she doing there, already frozen and all that way to swim back? Oh, would he never blow that damned whistle?

Stella slid into the water. The cold

was intense for a few moments. She saw her boat and aimed for alongside of it, keeping some six feet or so away, knowing that if she touched it she would be disqualified immediately. From the corners of her eyes she could just see their blurred figures, and the stem of the boat cutting through the water. When the other competitors were spread out and could not be seen it was comforting to glimpse the escort boat alongside. It was surprising how lonely it could seem in the middle of the lake.

Take it easy, she told herself, just to finish was all that mattered. A nice relaxed stroke — not too much leg kick, keep the beat slower and loosen the ankles — just enough to balance her and conserve energy. She could hear the rhythmic plunge of her hands into the water.

A touch of blue showed through the spray. Damn him, why did he have to come? If he had meant to upset her by being at the event he had succeeded. Suddenly the water seemed greyer, the sky darker. The events and troubles of the last weeks crowded into her mind. Carey was married. To someone called Estelle. Her mind took up the rhythm of her stroke. A married man — a married man — a married man.

With some apprehension she realised she was fading and not even halfway across. Her enthusiasm seemed to have waned, the cold was getting to her and her rhythm was beginning to go. Why not touch the boat, give up and let them pull her aboard? Did it matter now? Her crew were resting on their oars, gazing at her anxiously.

She fought herself. What about those friends and acquaintances of Carey's who could still be sponsoring her, the money which would so benefit the adoption society? Could she let them and the society down just because of a lover's quarrel? No, damn him! She would not allow thoughts of him to wreck her chance of getting across the lake. Perhaps that was what he wanted? Anger and native grit made her strike out with more determination to finish the course.

About a quarter of a mile to go and her limbs had lost their rhythm. The hotel behind the beach did not seem to be getting any nearer and it would be a miracle if she completed the swim. If only she could feel the pebbles beneath her feet. Now she realised that she should never have returned to Windermere as her mental attitude had not been right from the start. She was swimming almost blindly now, all cultured and thinking strokes gone. Nothing seemed to matter now. It seemed an awful effort even to turn her head, and water was getting into her mouth. Was the boat still with her? An irrational fear took hold of her. Perhaps she had drifted and they had lost her.

Her crew were leaning over towards her, smiling and shouting something and pointing ahead.

Through the splashing of her weary arms the faces appeared crescenting the beach. Her left hand touched bottom.

Kneeling in the water she tried to gain her feet, but the shifting surface of the shingle and the slight waves following her were enough to unbalance her. At the second attempt she made it upright.

Someone enclosed her in a large heavy towel. She heard murmurs of congratulations and tried to smile but her lips would hardly move. Just then all she wanted to do was get into the car, turn the heater on and warm herself thoroughly. Her crew having tied up the boat then began to escort her up the beach. Murmuring her thanks she croaked something about it being her slowest time ever. They could not know how much the seeing of *Fair Wind* had affected her. Of Carey's face dancing just above the lake water, tormenting and mocking her. She accompanied them unsteadily, depressed and drained.

Just as she reached the grass verge at the top of the beach, Stella felt their supporting hands leave her, and in their place two large warm enveloping ones held her shoulders from behind. The voice was unmistakable.

'May I offer my help? Congratulations Stella.'

Carey! Earlier it had gone through her mind that he might be there and she had made up her mind to ignore him. But now she was unable to and her resolve in her tired state was not as strong as it might have been. Turning slowly from under the shelter of the towel she looked up briefly into the face she had never expected to see again. 'Thank you,' she said stiffly.

'You will come for the presentation?'

'Presentation?' She couldn't think properly. Didn't he realise that she had just swum two miles in cold water? Then her memory was jolted. Of course, he meant the money for the society from the sponsors, and guessed that she would have to receive it on the society's behalf. 'Yes,' she nodded, 'I'll be there,' but didn't look at him again. He had chosen to speak to her when she was at her lowest ebb — she felt a million years old. Couldn't he have waited?

Her mind began to function more freely a few minutes later in the warmth of the car, and holding a hot cup of sweet tea with a dash of whisky in it. She was glad she had made the crossing — the money raised would benefit the adoption society, though halfway across she wouldn't have given anything for her chance of finishing.

Her thoughts ran on. She ought to have known that Carey would be there. She comforted herself by the fact that she need not stay any longer than necessary, just thank the sponsors and collect her certificate of completion. She smiled wryly. The time marked on it would be a joke as she must have taken twice as long as on the last occasion.

Stella then joined the other competitors and exchanged greetings and congratulations with those she knew. She wished that she could linger on awhile chatting to the other swimmers, and then either to go straight home, or to rest and warm oneself in an hotel or inn nearby. But this time was different for her. Carey and those who had sponsored her were watching and there was no way out. She had to face them and him again. They would remember her inelegant and hurried departure from Foxholme. She recognised some as they congratulated her, but she was conscious of the curiosity behind the smiles. They were trying to equate the half-drowned wretched figure that had emerged from the lake earlier with the well-dressed and groomed young woman they had met at the house.

There was no sign of Carey and she was glad in a way. Nevertheless the sight of him and his touch had unleashed the still strong fire of love she felt for him beneath the shock and anger of her discovery that he was married.

But then he appeared accompanied by an older man, Stella's eyes were drawn to Carey. Dressed immaculately and comfortably in fawn jacket and trousers, the white collar of his open-necked shirt emphasising his tan strongly. His eyes held hers momentarily, and trying to resist was difficult. He introduced his companion as Mr Redfern, secretary of the English Adoption Society.

Mr Redfern shook her hand. 'A very fine effort you put in there, Miss Bardon. You'll be pleased to know that your swim has raised the marvellous sum of just over eleven hundred pounds — so far.'

Eleven hundred pounds! That was unbelievable. The sponsors had been extremely generous. But what did he mean by so far? Was there more to come?

He looked around at the crowd. 'I think our entrant here deserves our congratulations,' and led a bout of clapping for her. Stella heard Carey clapping at her side and felt embarrassed and awkward with half the world it seemed looking on.

The secretary to the society spoke again. 'I think also we must pay tribute to your sponsors who have been absolutely splendid in their response to a worthy cause.'

Stella joined in the applause, then caught sight of a photographer hovering nearby. The event had never been like this before.

'However,' went on Mr Redfern, 'the society's good fortune is not over yet as Mr Carey Ganton here will explain. Thank you again.'

Stella felt her hand taken loosely in Carey's and drawn into the centre of those present. She recalled the time when she would have grasped his hand strongly in return, glorying in his vitality and attraction. Now her hand remained limply in his. In spite of this his resonant voice made her innermost being quiver when he spoke.

'One day earlier this year I made a promise to Miss Bardon.' What was the promise? To love her only, as he had whispered in the darkness of the four poster bed that night at Foxholme. She sighed inwardly, bitterly, as Carey continued. 'As some of you know I have a collection of old cars, and Miss Bardon showed a great interest when she saw them.'

Stella remembered their first kiss as they had stood by the side of one of the cars. What was he going to say next? Something to humiliate her and show her up in front of all those people?

'Well, ladies and gentlemen, Miss Bardon has crossed the lake, she has fulfilled her part of the agreement, and now it is my turn. I promised that she could choose any car in the collection and that I would offer it for auction — the proceeds going to the society chosen by her.' Applause broke out as he paused.

In some confusion Stella recalled their conversation. They had been dancing together when he had told her of his decision.

Carey was speaking again. 'Now, I just happen to know which car she likes,' and he glanced at her with eyes which had once been warmly enveloping, but now held a distant amusement. 'But being a woman she could have changed her mind.'

Stella managed to return a tight little smile. 'So I guess I've taken a risk in bringing that particular one. Shall we go and start the bidding?' He turned upwards from the beach, the crowd giving way to let them through.

Where was he taking her? She gasped. Standing at the kerb was the pink and maroon car she had last seen in the garage at Foxholme. Even then in those strained circumstances that she found herself in, she had to admit that the vehicle was staggeringly beautiful — a car from another age posing elegantly in the summer evening.

She watched in a daze as Carey conducted the auction, the price creeping up. He then asked her to sit in it, behaving as if nothing had ever been wrong between them. She put on a fixed smile and tried to look as if she were enjoying the occasion as admirers and bidders jostled around. She was glad when the bidding was over, the car sold and she could get out. But one thing she had to admit and that was that he had kept his word.

When Stella heard of the full amount that had been raised she could hardly believe it — most of it coming from the proceeds of the car auction. She was thrilled for the society as the money would set them in credit for years to come.

But Stella's ordeal was not over yet. Just as she thought they would not require her any more and that she might slip away, the photographer said, 'Now how about a shot of you and Mr Ganton by the car? Sponsor and sponsored as you might say.' She was trapped. People were already gathered around to watch.

'Can you get closer together,' requested the photographer, 'and smile please, Miss Bardon.'

Carey moved until he was touching

her and glanced down at her. 'Surely you can pretend you're enjoying my company just for a few seconds,' he whispered sideways. His voice was hard.

Stella was cold, miserable inside. That voice had not so very long ago said it had loved her.

'Relax and smile please.' Even the cameraman must have noticed it. They were acting out a scene — it was unreal to Stella, and all she had feared would happen had done so. Coming up for the swim had been a terrible mistake. With relief she saw the photographer move aside, but was surprised when those around continued to gaze expectantly at her.

Carey moved away a little but kept hold of her hand. 'I think they're waiting for you to say something. I hope they get more from you than I have.'

She looked at the faces in dismay. Never had she felt her less like making a speech, but other people besides Carey were involved and she owed them her thanks for their support. Forcing herself to smile at them, she said, 'Just to thank you all — those who sponsored me and had faith in me, although at one stage during the swim I think I had less faith that I should finish than you did probably. For some reason or other I lost it a bit halfway across.' If only they knew why. 'I'm very pleased for the society that so much money has been raised.' She glanced sideways at Carey — stern and sombre faced, standing arms folded and gazing down at the pebbles. 'I must also add my thanks to Mr Ganton,' — she nearly said Carey — 'for his magnificent gesture in donating the car for the auction.' Finding a smile, she added, 'And he was quite right, it was my favourite one. Thank you.' She turned away after the clapping, relieved beyond measure that it was all over.

Carey was still standing by the car, and without ignoring him completely it was difficult not to meet his gaze. 'Goodnight,' she murmured, feeling awkward and sad and not really sure what she wanted to happen next. Perhaps it would be better if she joined those going across the road to the car park and not look back.

'Stella.' The voice came before she'd gone two yards. It was commanding, yet held a plea.

Don't be a fool, keep going, her mind yelled. Just be polite and call goodbye over her shoulder.

'Stella — please.' A little of the pride had gone from the sound compared with the first call.

Stella halted and half turned. Once already in their relatively short acquaintance she had tasted the power of his assault upon her senses. It had been an earthquake in her life. 'I have to go, my friends are waiting in the car.' Her manner was offhand — deliberately so. She must keep him at arms' length.

Carey stopped a few feet from her. 'You didn't reply to my letter I wrote you. Did you get it?' he demanded.

She glanced at him and away again

quickly, 'Yes, I got it.'

'Well then.' She heard the frown in his tone and guessed his eyes were waiting to probe hers if she looked up.

'I tore it up — I didn't read it. I — I must go now.'

'You didn't read it?' He was silent for a few moments, and Stella gained a pale satisfaction. It must have been a shock to him to find a woman who had not even bothered to read what he had written. No doubt he had been used to them hanging around the door for the mail or hovering over the phone.

'You didn't look at it at all?'

'No.'

'But I explained everything. So that's why you won't have anything to do with me.' There was relief in his voice.

'I don't want your explanations by letter or otherwise. I found out all I wanted to know last time,' and her voice was as cold as the lake water, greying in the after sun. Only by the merest narrowing of his eyes and tautening of his cheeks did Carey reveal that her words had affected him.

He continued to look at her, then said evenly, 'How about us going somewhere together for dinner or a drink. We can talk. I think you owe me that at least.' He took a step nearer to her.

She almost stumbled in her anxiety not to allow him to touch her. Her resistance would crumble and her passion flare from the embers of a love that had not yet left her.

Carey looked shocked and shrugged slightly. 'Hell, Stella, you must hate me.'

'No, I don't hate you, Carey.' She could never do that, she knew now. She managed to stare straight into his face. 'And you're right, I do owe you. I'm grateful for the effort you made tonight. You kept your word about donating the car — I didn't think you would. I was wrong, it was a big gesture and I thank you.'

'Oh, damn the donation and society. I did it because of you — only you. I wanted to see you again, and if I've done some good for your society, all right, so be it. You know damn well I can afford it anyway. Give me a chance to tell you what was in the letter that you didn't read.'

Stella's emotions were being torn apart, but there could be no future with a married man. The truth was that she would retain a scar of love for the remainder of her life. 'It was a dream — a marvellous dream, Carey, but it was spoiled for me.' Taking a deep breath she went on, 'I'm getting over it now.' It was a lie but she did not want him to see that she was still carrying a torch for him. 'So let's just leave it at that.'

'We can't leave it like that. I meant those things that I said that night. I asked you to marry me then — I still want you to do now, nothing's changed.' Carey's voice was strongly persuasive and reasoning.

Past his shoulder Stella was aware of the new owner of the auctioned car still busy admiring his purchase. A sudden great and miserable sadness overcame her. This emotion fuelled an anger already welling up inside her that things had gone so horribly wrong. She and Carey should be in that car, beginning to drive away from the kerb and perhaps taking them to Foxholme for dinner.

'How can you say that?' she burst out furiously. 'You're married, and I'm not going to be a partner in bigamy.' She stared fiercely out of a distraught face. 'I suppose you thought I was a soft touch.'

His nostrils flared, the anger flickered in his piercing gaze. 'Don't tell me you were not just a little attracted by the aura of the rich,' and his tone was scathing.

Stella was hurt and it showed. 'Maybe, but you'd have been the same to me without your possessions.' She was conscious of people glancing at them curiously, and determined that she would try and keep some dignity. She began to turn away.

Suddenly his hand had gripped her arm, making her wince. 'Wait,' he ordered. 'In that case come back to Foxholme with me, and between us we'll straighten things out. Don't let's spoil it, Stella.'

Stella tried to pull away. 'You're hurting me — let me go.'

He did and she stared at him panting — her upper body heaving with her emotions. 'What you really mean,' she flung at him, 'is don't let me spoil your fun. All you want is somebody — and I mean some body to take to bed with you. Maybe you thought I was a good time girl. Well, if so, this is one that's throwing you over.' She wanted to hurt him as he had hurt her. People were staring at them as she stormed on. 'Take your wife back to Foxholme, straighten things out between you and her, that's what you should do. And where is she today? Where is she any day? Or are you hiding her whilst you do your philandering?'

Stella saw the swiftly rising terrible

anger in Carey's face. He swallowed, his hands opening and closing quickly at his sides, his dark brows knitted as one. Suddenly she was in a grip of iron again. A look of pain screwed up his features, and she was shocked at the tormenting emotions let loose there. After what seemed an eternity he regained some composure, leaving only his eyes to rake her face with an intensity that left her in no doubt as to the power of his feelings.

His voice when it came was a choking groan. 'You damn silly little fool. You ask me where my wife is. I'll tell you where she is.' His lips had disappeared leaving only a slit. 'She's dead, by God, she's dead. Do you understand, you bitch? Dead — dead a year.' He shook her once savagely as the volcano within himself neared eruption, then let her go abruptly to turn swiftly and leave her.

When she had regained her balance Carey was already getting into the passenger seat of the maroon and pink roadster. Stunned by what she had just been told, Stella stared after him. Her arm shot out in his direction as if by doing that she could summon him back — a futile hopeless gesture.

The car ignition fired and then the machine was passing her. Carey grim and granite-faced, staring ahead, with not the merest glance her way, and the driver, the new owner, glancing at her curiously as they swept by.

Too late Stella found some voice — an inarticulate cry after Carey's fast disappearing back. A tiny unimportant sound swallowed up in the noise and borne away by the uncaring breeze.

How long she sat on the lakeside seat she did not know. It didn't matter; nothing mattered now. Quiet tears ran in the dark as she drove home. She had meant to stop for a celebration drink on the return, but there was nothing for her to celebrate. The completion of the swim was insignificant after what had happened between Carey and herself.

8

That night in the darkness of her bed, her mind persisted cruelly in recalling what had happened. What a monumental idiot she had been — an impetuous childlike fool, jumping to the wrong conclusions, too eager and willing to believe the worst of Carey. The look on his face which she would never forget when he had informed her that his wife was dead. The things that she, Stella, had said to the man who had asked for her hand in marriage. How awful it must have been for him. She curled and cringed inside herself. Why, oh why had she not read his letter, or listened for just a few seconds longer on the phone instead of cutting him off?

What a little miss prim and proper she had been, and at a time when he needed comforting and solace. He had made love to her a year after his wife had died. Was that so much of a crime? The truth was that she had set herself up as his judge and condemned him without a trial. But what had Carey's wife died from? Had it been some dread disease or an accident? And had he loved her? He must have done, otherwise he would not have married her. But then Stella recalled what Kindon Ferrers had told her about it being a strange marriage and that he did not believe that Carey loved his wife.

Stella turned restlessly in bed and thumped the pillow. It mattered nothing now.

Outside, the wind had risen strongly about the house, rattling the windows — a fitting moaning orchestration to accompany her abject misery. In the morning she determined to phone Carey and apologise for her shameful behaviour.

Nervously Stella waited after dialling, but it was a woman — Florence the housekeeper whom Stella remembered meeting. 'Could I speak to Mr Ganton please.'

'Sorry Miss Bardon, but he's not here. I just don't know where he is.' There was a trace of anxiety in the housekeeper's voice. 'He did come in for a short time last evening, but he didn't seem himself at all. Just straight in and out again, and he wouldn't have anything to eat. I haven't seen him since. I hope he's not sickening for something.'

'Oh, I'm sure he'll be all right, Florence,' said Stella, trying to sound cheerful, but finding it very hard.

'Well, I've never seen such a change in him before. When he left in the afternoon he was in good spirits, a bit thoughtful but nothing like he was when he returned. I don't know what happened to make him like that.'

But I do, thought Stella miserably, and it was all her fault.

Florence sounded worried when she spoke again. 'We had a bad night up here, Miss Bardon. The weather changed and it was very wild and stormy.'

'And he's been away all night?'

'Yes, I'm beginning to wonder what's happened. When he's going to be away he usually tells me, and then I know when to expect him back, so's I can prepare a meal.'

'Perhaps he's just forgotten.' Stella made an attempt to reassure the other although she felt she had little to offer anyone in the way of comfort at that moment.

'I suppose that's it. Shall I tell Mr Ganton that you phoned?'

Stella thought quickly. She did not want the housekeeper to know that she and Carey had quarrelled. Her apologies must be made personally and not through another person. 'No thanks Florence, I'd rather you didn't. I'll ring again later.'

Stella sighed with tension and frustration as she hung up. So he'd been out all night, and it was all her fault. The things she had said and the way she had said them had been enough to drive a man to do anything. She pictured his expression again as he had left her. Florence had no need to worry about his whereabouts that wild night, because no doubt he had done what he had been told to do, and that was to find another female companion with a more sympathetic ear than Stella's had been. Bitterness gnawed away at her.

The day dragged on at her school. How she managed to get through it she would never know. Usually for the twenty-four hours following the swim she was lethargic, but the quarrel with Carey on top of that had left her deeply and hopelessly despairing. She decided that she would try again to contact him as soon as she got home from work.

In the staff common room at lunch time Phyllis, a colleague remarked, 'It's lucky for you that the swim wasn't scheduled for today.'

'Oh why?' The tired and dulled eyes opposite had brightened briefly.

'I just caught it on the radio — a

violent storm over Cumbria during the night. Roads awash, trees down, and boats dragging their moorings — a real mess. I think around Windermere got the worst of the storm.'

It had been a stormy evening in more than one way, thought Stella bitterly.

Nevertheless, the first thing she did when she returned home was to switch the television on for the northern news. Watching disinterestedly as the industrial news was given, she knew that she was making it an excuse to delay phoning Carey with her apologies. She decided to make a cup of tea. Just as she was adding the milk the newscaster's voice penetrated into the kitchen ' . . . worst storm in living memory . . . ' Stella hurried back into the room to gaze in shock at the scene of devastation being shown. ' . . . North-west England and particularly the Lake District suffered. The cost of the damage is estimated to run into millions of pounds.' Abandoned cars, trees across roads and boats torn from their moorings.

The camera ranged over the grey and still unsettled waters of the lake. Upturned boats and some lying on their sides on the banks. Then followed the close-up of a blue hull half submerged and on its side inshore. Stella stared rigidly at the wreck as the voice of the newscaster went on, 'Some concern is being felt for the whereabouts of Mr Carey Ganton, owner of the yacht *Fair Wind* shown here. Mr Ganton is thought to have been aboard during the storm but as yet no trace of him has been found. Mr Ganton has only just recently settled in Windermere. He is the chairman and founder of the Sunside Yacht Co. of America, and is himself an experienced yachtsman. Yesterday he donated an old car from his valuable collection after the annual cross-lake swim in aid of the English Adoption and Orphan Society — a record sum of money was raised. It is estimated that it will be several days before . . . '

But Stella wasn't listening. A devil mocked inwardly — she would have no need to telephone and apologise now. Fears pressed themselves upon her, each one conjuring up a picture worse than the last. Carey had not returned home last night, she knew that from the housekeeper. In the angry state he was in when he had left her Stella knew that he was capable of anything. The yacht had meant a great deal to him. Had he taken it out to try to find solace and peace of mind on the water? Her final fear was too terrible to give thought to, but the picture of the wreck had imprinted itself mercilessly upon her mind. She sought comfort in the thought that perhaps after all he had not been aboard last night and was even now at home or on his way there. Doubt soon returned. Why, if he was all right, had he not contacted someone during the last few hours?

Grabbing the telephone she dialled

Foxholme. The worried voice of Florence told her that there had been no news yet of Mr Ganton, and she was beginning to fear the worst. Stella put the phone down, feeling confused and helpless. But what could she do? Almost before the question had formed in her mind, she knew. There was no way she could spend the next few hours alone torturing herself with thoughts about what had happened to Carey.

Stopping only long enough to fling on a coat, she headed her car for Windermere. Somehow she must find out where Carey was even if . . . Stella shook her head as if to shake the dreadful thought that he might have drowned. Why couldn't he be wandering concussed somewhere with a loss of memory after swimming ashore? She drove as fast as traffic and conditions would allow. Her brain was busy — feverishly so. He had asked her to marry him and she loved him and must find him. He needed help now and she must not fail him again.

Her imagination reproduced the picture of *Fair Wind* as she had seen it on the news. And surely that had been the ferry terminal for the western side of the lake she had seen as the camera had moved in? Stella decided to make straight for that spot.

When she arrived it was dull and grey with a light rain falling. The lake was sullen looking, brooding after its violence of a few hours before. The ferry was running and impatiently she waited for it to return from the other side. How slowly it moved towards her. On the way over she strained her eyes anxiously as the western side of the lake drew nearer. There was plenty of activity it appeared going on with figures moving on the shore in front of what was now becoming clear to Stella as a large blue-hulled yacht on its side in the water. Usually on a fine day there would be about half a dozen craft swinging at moorings near there, but now a few upturned small craft kept it company like a beached whale with its young.

Her car charged off the ferry and over the ramp to screech to a halt near the path which ran along the lakeside to the north of the terminal. Out of the car and dashing along the path she prayed. Frogmen in flippers were grouped on the foreshore, whilst more were busy in the water with ropes around the yacht. Those on shore turned at her approach, observing her very obvious distress.

'Mr Ganton — Mr Ganton,' she gasped breathlessly, 'have you found him yet?' Fear stared out of her eyes. 'This is *Fair Wind* isn't it?'

The nearest replied to her first question. 'It's all right, we've found no-one. There was no-one on board.'

Great relief filled her. 'Oh, thank God,' she breathed. 'Has there been any news of him?' But no-one could say, and Stella glanced at *Fair Wind* lying with its deck and cockpit facing her. How graceful and proud it had been once. The cockpit, where she and Carey had sat together above the warm blue seas of that island, and then on the lake in happier times. The interior which had echoed with laughter on the sunny lazy afternoon of the house party and when the deck had been alive with bronzed and happy guests — she had been one of them. The masts, one of them broken, reached out from the water on to the beach as if for help, and Stella remembered how their tips had swayed across the southern blue sky, tracing the message of love that had so suddenly been awakened in her.

She stumbled away, uncaring of the curious stares of the bystanders. But then a new fear lanced her, replacing the other. They had not found him in the yacht, that was true, but that did not mean that he could not have been drowned away from it — thrown into the water as it capsized. Please God, don't let it be. She must think positively and discipline her emotions.

She slumped into her car seat and stared desperately through the screen.

Supposing he was still alive and suffering from loss of memory, lost in the country-side or even lying injured in some out of the way place. Maybe he had stumbled into a farm or had been taken into some household. Her mind rejected this reluctantly. Surely those giving him shelter would by now have heard the news and telephoned the police or Carey's home for someone to come and collect him. It was quite possible also that in the time she had taken to get to Windermere he had been found and taken to Foxholme or hospital. It might be a good idea if she found out before searching any further. There was an inn she remembered about a mile along the road ahead, and she could telephone from there to Foxholme. Glancing at her watch she saw there was only an hour before the last ferry back to Bowness. But what did that matter? If Carey had not returned home she must carry on searching for him.

The Pigeon and Partridge was busy

but Stella found the phone and waited feverishly. Florence replied in very upset tones, saying there had been no word from him and that the police had contacted her, but Carey had not been admitted to any hospital.

Sadly and hopelessly Stella hung up and glanced around, seeing the warm subdued lighting, and people enjoying themselves. Hearing laughter with couples standing close to each other and young people in corners of dark wood speaking into each other's faces — in love. She and Carey should have been in some place together that night. He would not need to speak; the look in his eyes would reveal all that he felt for her. Stella passed a miserable and weary hand across her forehead. Instead she was chasing round the countryside like a demented thing looking for the man she had ordered out of her life twenty four hours earlier.

She found the landlord, and gave a description of Carey and his name. The landlord looked sympathetically at the dishevelled and anxious-faced girl across the bar. 'If only I had, m'dear. I've heard about it. The police have been here before you. I told them the same. Sorry — wish I could help.'

Stella returned to the deepening dusk outside. That meant that probably they had visited the other inns in the district. Nevertheless, she knew that she must find out for herself and would not rest until she had.

But it was the same story, elsewhere. No-one answering his description had booked in or had been seen. Stella kept on searching, driving slowly and peering in the fading light into driveways, courtyards and farmyards. Memories returned vividly. There was the road she and Carey had taken to Hawkshead when they had dined at the White Horse. That spring day when everything had been nearly perfect. She realised now that she had held for a brief period the slippery transient emotion called happiness. It was when she and Carey in *Fair Wind* had gently drifted down the lake and afterwards there was the lovely surprise of being driven to Hawkshead in his open car. At the time it had seemed that nature had given its seal of approval to their blossoming friendship as they had glided over this very road.

Stella sighed bitterly. If only fate could have made a small magnanimous gesture to her and let her find out that he was unmarried. Her thoughtless impetuosity and holier than thou attitude had ruined everything. As far as she knew there was not another inn or hotel until Hawkshead. And why should that place hold any more hope in her quest to find Carey than the others? All she could think of was that it was the one place where they had dined together. A wild piece of illogical reasoning she realised, but she must try every hunch in her efforts to find him. A bottomless despair filled her as she drove on urgently and the road seemed endless as if it had taken on more curves and corners to hinder her desperate dash.

It was nearly dark when she arrived in the narrow street of Hawkshead village. A police car was parked outside the White Horse Inn. Stella pulled up in front of it and stumbled out, the smell of cooking wafting to her as she glanced at the window behind which she and Carey had sat that night. It had been a carefree, beautiful evening when he had caressed her with his eyes and voice, and they had talked and told each other about themselves. And if he was not found soon then the nightmare that he was dead would come true.

Pushing the door open Stella stepped inside, heartache intensifying when she recalled how she had warned him about the low beams inside the inn. He had chuckled with wonder and delight at the inviting interior of the old world place, and had assumed an exaggerated stoop to clear them. How wonderful it had been, and only now did she realise just how wonderful. This place had to provide her with some hope — it had to as she didn't think she could go on any longer. Her eyes were drawn to the corner table by the window — their table.

She felt some surprise at not seeing a policeman in the building as the police car was parked right outside. Making a great effort to firm her voice, she asked, 'I — I am looking for a Mr Carey Ganton — an American. He's tall and he's been missing since last night. I wondered if he had called in here.' Her gaze was unwavering, alert to anything on the other's face which would give her hope for Carey's survival.

The barman hesitated, frowned. 'Ganton,' he said slowly. 'I seem to have heard that name. Problem is I wasn't here during the day. Why don't . . . ' The fair-haired girl in the bronze jump suit behind the bar who had just served a customer suddenly pointed past Stella's right shoulder. 'There, that's him coming down now. The police have come to take him home. Poor fellow lost his boat — arrived last night. Been up there in his room all the time.'

Stella whirled wide-eyed, indescribable joy and relief exploding in her heart and plain on her face. It was! It was Carey reaching the foot of the stairs. Oh, Carey! Her Carey, alive and safe, with a policeman on one side, a ginger-haired casually dressed man on the other, the latter having a steadying hand on Carey's arm.

She started forward, her weary misery forgotten, her brain registering his ill-fitting clothing. He looked like a man who had just awakened and dressed in a hurry. 'Carey. Oh Carey, I'm so glad you're all right. I've looked everywhere for you. I was so afraid.' She was alongside them. There would be time to apologise later in full, but just to see him was enough.

She saw him hesitate and slow down, but he kept moving and the glance he gave her was dull, disinterested, that of a stranger. Her first reaction was that he just did not recognise her. She knew that she must look pretty awful.

The trio continued towards the door, and Stella hurried after them oblivious and uncaring of the turning heads and stares. 'Carey,' she called, 'it's Stella — wait.'

She saw the policeman touch Carey on the sleeve. 'The young lady wants to speak to you sir. She seems to know you.'

Carey turned slowly to face her and Stella observed his haggard and unshaven features. All would be well when she explained and apologised, she was sure. Those people within earshot had gone quiet. She smiled for the first time in the past twenty four hours and words tumbled out in her relief. 'Oh thank God, Carey, you're alive. I thought all sorts of things. I've searched high and low for you and I've nearly gone mad. I saw the boat on television — came as quickly as I could. I didn't know where you were. This was going to be the last place. Please forgive me for what I said yesterday. I'd no idea.'

The hazel eyes which had caressed her so warmly on other occasions now looked through her. There was recognition but nothing else, and when he spoke his tone was indifferent and lacking in vitality. 'Please don't bother me. I don't know you — I don't want to know who you are, and I don't care.'

The nightmare descended on Stella again. She felt as if she were in a film scene for two actors, caught in some awful tableau waiting to be freed from it — waiting for the director to say 'take five'. Carey shouldn't be saying those words — they were the wrong ones. Instead he should be delighted and welcoming, asking how she had been and how great to see her. Sure, he'd forgotten already about the quarrel — the things she had said — and he didn't blame her. Certainly he'd been upset and stayed the night at the inn. As for the storm, hell, what did it matter about his boat as long as they had found each other again.

Part of her mind struggled to

convince the rest of it that that was how he really felt, but seeing him turn away and go through the doorway with the others shattered that idea. Catching the door just before it closed, she stumbled out after them.

Light from the inn's windows and the lamp above its door showed Carey bending into the car, the policeman about to close the door on him. 'Carey,' she cried despairingly, 'you do know me. You can't have forgotten me — you loved me.' For the moment Stella's pride had gone. 'Please come back, Carey.'

From inside the car the policeman put out a gently halting hand at her. 'Sorry miss, Mr Ganton doesn't know you. I should go back inside if I were you, miss.' His tone was admonishing but kindly as if talking to an irksome child.

'No, wait, he's lying.' Her voice was stretched and cracked. 'You don't understand, he was going to marry me. We had a quarrel and then . . . ' She tailed off and even in the semi darkness the policeman's understanding was revealed all too clearly by his expression.

'I'm afraid they all say that, miss,' he said with some sympathy.

Unbelievingly and sick to her soul Stella stared as his arm disappeared as he shut the car door. 'It wasn't like that.' She choked on her words. 'We loved each other.' It began to move off and she could see the outline of Carey's head through the rear window which moved neither left nor right. She stood as if hypnotised until the rear lights vanished from view.

Confusion was rampant in Stella's mind as she fell deeper and deeper into an abyss of abject misery. She had found him but at what cost to her heart. It would have been better if she had never seen him again and joyful memories might have sustained her. That way this last bitter slashing of those lovely memories of their good times together would have been avoided.

The agony of mind, the stresses and strains that she had endured were too much for Stella, and with a sighing sob she crumpled to the ground — the cruel world mercifully blotted out for a short time.

9

When Stella came to she found herself lying on a couch and two faces looking down on her wearing a mixture of anxiety and curiosity. One of them she recognised as being the red-haired man who had escorted Carey from the inn with the policeman, and a plump auburn haired woman — his wife Teresa, the owners of the inn. They had brought Stella into their private quarters after she had fainted.

'I thought you might have hurt your head on the ground when you fainted,' said Alec the husband.

Stella managed a wan smile. 'I'm sorry — I think I made a fool of myself.'

He smiled her apology away. 'Don't worry, these things happen.'

'How do you feel now?' asked his wife.

'Oh, not too bad thank you. I'll be all right.' Actually she felt awful, empty and at rock bottom mentally and physically.

'Now you stay here and rest. I'm going to get you a nice strong cup of tea.'

Stella nodded wearily, gratefully, and leaned back, unable to think straight and not even wanting to.

After bringing the tea Teresa surveyed her with sympathetic understanding.

'Man trouble was it?' she asked gently.

Stella nodded despairingly. 'Yes, it's all gone wrong. We quarrelled, but he'd no right to ignore me. Anyway it's done now — over,' she finished hopelessly.

'I'm sorry,' said Alec's wife, then regarded the younger woman speculatively. 'Would you like to talk about it? Sometimes it helps.'

Stella glanced up at her. Teresa was a stranger and knew nothing of her, yet sometimes it was easier to tell your troubles to a stranger than it was to someone closer. 'But I don't want to burden you with my problems, and anyway you must be a very busy person.'

Teresa shook her head. 'I don't mind, go ahead. It's an excuse for me to get away from work for a while. They'll have to manage without me for once.'

A memory came suddenly, painfully to Stella. 'Carey and I dined here once earlier this year. It was wonderful.' Her eyes had misted over. Was real love always like this? Did you have to pay so dearly for such a short measure of happiness?

Teresa spoke with a little smile. 'And did you enjoy your meal?'

Dry bread would have been a banquet eaten in his company. She realised that whether she had enjoyed the meal itself obviously meant a great deal to the kind person opposite her. 'It was lovely, thank you, and I shall always remember it.'

The face brightened with pleasure. 'Oh, I'm glad,' but then its owner sighed. 'It's not easy running a place like this. So many regulations nowadays, we don't get much time off.' She paused and smiled rather sadly. 'And time goes by.' Her gaze flickering over Stella. 'But you're young — you have plenty of time.' She nodded knowingly. 'There'll be others.'

There would never be another Carey, thought Stella despondently. He had brought love to her, then that heaven had been snatched away from her, and now she was back in the real world where things didn't happen just as you wanted them to. Briefly she went on to tell the older woman of how she had met Carey and subsequent happenings between them.

In turn she found out that Teresa had heard of some wealthy American buying Foxholme with the intention of settling in the district. 'I think it's a lovely romantic story and I really feel for you; there's an article about him in the local paper tonight. There's a picture of him donating that car to the charity.' Teresa eyed Stella contemplatively. 'Seems to me that if he asked you to marry him he must have been in love with you.'

Stella regarded her companion hopelessly. 'Then I went and made a mess of things after that sponsored swim.'

'He must be a very generous person to have done that. I think people always expect a rich person to give money away, but I don't agree with that. His was a lovely gesture, giving such a car. I think it must have meant a lot to him.'

Stella looked down into the last of her tea as the landlord's wife added, 'From what I saw of him he was quite a dish; I'm not surprised you fell for him. Maybe he'll get in touch with you again. If it's not another woman and from what you've told me it isn't, then I think there's a chance.' Teresa's voice was cheerfully optimistic.

'I don't think so, Teresa, but thanks,' and there was so much certainty in Stella's that it dismissed any hope of that happening.

The other nodded at her empty cup. 'Would you like another — maybe with something stronger in it?'

Stella accepted the offer with a wry but grateful smile. 'Thanks, and maybe something to put me out forever.'

'Now we can't have that sort of talk,' said Teresa frowning sternly but kindly as she left. On returning she sat next to Stella on the couch whilst the latter drank the mixture of tea and whisky — half and half she guessed, but anything to dull the pain of mind.

'I've been thinking about this Carey of yours, and I wouldn't take it for granted that he won't come round after a while,' said Teresa.

'Oh.' A flicker of interest stirred out of the deep depression. Her eyes met the other woman's then slid away.

'Well, I'm not taking sides,' went on Teresa, 'but he can't have been feeling too good himself. Perhaps you just caught him at a bad time. I know he was in a rough state yesterday, and I'm sure that when he's recovered he'll regret what's happened.'

How simple and easy she made it sound, thought Stella. Teresa was trying to cheer her up she knew, but the rift between Carey and herself had widened further at their last brief meeting. Stella couldn't bring herself to believe that their love affair would blossom again; it was over.

'Might be a good idea to give him a day or two to get over things,' suggested the older woman. 'After all he's lost his boat and quarrelled with you, and then why not contact him — phone him — pay him a visit?'

Stella gazed at her very doubtfully. 'It's great of you to try and help and I appreciate it, Teresa, but I've no right to involve you. Maybe there is something in what you say though I just can't see it happening like that.'

All the same the idea lingered in Stella's mind. She had nothing to lose now, only what was left of her pride, and there was precious little of that. Perhaps it was the whisky taking effect but she heard herself asking, 'When did Carey get here?' She was puzzled as to why he had stayed on all that day at the inn?

Teresa pondered a moment. 'About nine thirty last night, and the weather was terrible. He looked a mess, soaked to the skin and wild looking. I didn't know who he was and he didn't say at first, just wanted a room. I guessed he was an American. We had one vacant, so we let him have it. In any case we couldn't turn him away on a night like that.'

'So he'd swum ashore from the boat then?' No wonder he was in such a state, thought Stella, but was surprised when Teresa shook her head. 'No, he told us later that he anchored his boat near the ferry terminal when the storm was getting up, then just walked here.' She gave a puzzled shrug. 'Alec and I just couldn't understand it. He didn't seem to care.'

Stella stared in amazement at her. So he hadn't been in the boat when it went down. She remembered her fears for his safety, her desperate journey north to find him and the circumstances she now found herself in. Anger flared in her. And then he had treated her like dirt. God! if only she'd known.

'It was only this evening when he found out that his boat had been wrecked.' Teresa informed her.

Stella couldn't keep up her anger, being too tired and confused, and there was so much that she didn't understand. 'But why did he stay here so long?' Mystified she concentrated on Teresa's face.

'Because my dear,' stated that person simply, 'he was incapable of going anywhere — doing anything. He was drunk.'

'Drunk!' exclaimed Stella incredulously.

Teresa waved a hand. 'Oh no, not when he arrived, but within a short time of being in the place. He had a bath and we loaned him some clothes, then he ordered a bottle in his room. It

181

didn't stop there though, he had more. I was frightened that he might kill himself with the stuff, I was thankful when he just fell asleep.' She paused reflectively before continuing, 'I was very surprised because he struck me as being a man who would know how much he could take — someone with finer tastes. I just couldn't understand it then but having heard your story I think I do now.' Going on she said, 'During the night Alec kept a watch on him, and he said that your friend had been rambling on about someone called Stella, called her a bitch — mentioned the name a lot.' She smiled wonderingly. 'You must have made quite an impression on him.'

'But not the right kind, judging by the way he treated me tonight,' replied Stella bitterly.

'Well, maybe as I said, he may feel better towards you later. He'd only just sobered up before you arrived — slept most of the day. I don't think we've seen a man get drunk so quickly as your friend did last night. But it was deliberate — that was obvious. He just wanted to blot out everything.'

So that was why he had looked so rough and not at all like the Carey she had known.

'Later,' Teresa informed her, 'he told me who he was and then we saw the local paper and realised that there was a search on for him. He told us to ring the police and his home, and as you know the police came for him.'

Yes, she did know and would never forget the incident. But she must make an effort now and get back home, though dreading the thought of the journey. She pushed herself to her feet. 'Thanks for everything Teresa, but I'd better start for home now, otherwise the last ferry will have gone, and besides I've taken up enough of your time.'

Teresa looked concerned. 'The last ferry went an hour ago, and it's a long way round by road,' she pointed out, 'and anyway I don't think you're fit to go anywhere tonight. Why don't you stay here? We'll find a room for you. You've had a shock and it's late and I wouldn't like to think of you being on the roads tonight.'

Stella acquiesced. It was all too easy to do so and no more persuasion by her kindly companion was necessary. The thought of work came and went swiftly as it was beyond her ability at present to cope with it. She was drifting in a state of shock, waiting as it were for some sort of order and reason to be restored inside herself. Life appeared to hold very little for her at that particular moment.

Teresa found her a single room, brought her sandwiches, more tea and night clothes. 'What we did for your Carey we can do for you,' she stated with a brisk cheerfulness.

Afterwards with the night covering her, the words 'your Carey' hung and danced white and mocking before Stella's eyes. Her Carey. Once for a fraction of time that had been true. Then as the inn grew quiet Stella slipped into sleep, exhaustion blunting the heartache. And in the place where they had once dined and enjoyed each other's company malicious fate had ordered that she be alone just as he had been the night before.

She was awakened in the morning by Teresa bringing breakfast and Stella wondered how she could repay this hospitable woman and her husband. Perhaps when this awful period in her life was over she would find some way. Memories of the last night's events tried to crowd into her consciousness as she sipped at her tea. She glanced through the window as if to avoid confrontation with them, seeing that it was sunny and the branches dancing in the summer morning's breeze.

She could feel the sun's rays warming her legs through the bedcovers, and subdued noises from elsewhere in the building came to her. It was peaceful and relaxing, and she allowed herself to think rationally about what had happened over the last two days, not only to herself but also to Carey.

After the swim they had quarrelled and she had gone home, and Carey had driven off, and had returned to Foxholme, and then left again very soon afterwards. He must have gone straight to the yacht and taken it out on to the lake. He had tried to find peace and consolation alone on the water. Afterwards when the storm blew up he had anchored and come ashore, then walked to the inn. Had he been drawn to it by the memory of that happy few hours they had spent there together? Some feeling for her must have remained in him. Once there he had attempted to drown his problems in drink, and by all accounts had succeeded for a day.

After she had bathed and dressed Stella stood gazing out of the window. With the brighter weather had come a definite uplift in her spirits. As Teresa had said, Carey would have had time to think and would perhaps be in a better frame of mind. She had suggested that

Stella ring him or see him after a few days. But another idea was forming in the latter's mind. Why wait until then? Why not speak to him whilst she was already in the district? Just a few words spoken calmly over the phone. They might serve to break the barrier between Carey and herself. It was worth a try.

She day-dreamed. They would apologise together. He might even invite her up to the house. Then along with this steady surge of optimism came a more daring thought. The phone was a cold and impersonal thing — the tone of voice could be misinterpreted. Would it not be better to go up to Foxholme that very day?

Downstairs Teresa and Alec were surprised when they saw her. 'Well, I must say the rest has certainly done you good, Stella,' exclaimed Teresa, looking her over as if seeing her for the first time. 'That Carey of yours wants his head examining if he doesn't get in touch with you again.'

'I'm not going to give him the chance not to,' announced Stella. 'I've taken your advice, Teresa, and I'm going to contact him myself today. As soon as I leave here I'm going to Foxholme — where he lives. We can work something out I'm sure.'

The sudden look of doubt on Teresa's face went unnoticed by Stella as she bent over her purse. 'You've been the kindest people I shall ever meet, and I'm so grateful for everything you've done for me.'

They waved her offer away.

'I just hope the two of you get together again, and if you do please invite us to the wedding,' said a smiling Teresa.

'Oh, I'll do that don't you worry,' Stella said with great feeling, then added with an optimistic cheerfulness unknown to her for the last two days, 'and don't forget to reserve that corner table for us.'

She kissed Teresa gratefully on the cheek and shook hands with Alec. 'I'll phone you as soon as possible. Keep your fingers crossed for me.' Then waving goodbye to them she drove off, unaware of Teresa's anxious frown and doubtful shake of her head as she and her husband re-entered the White Horse.

Stella headed for the ferry. The morning was warm, bright and the country road busy; such a contrast in every way to the day before. Her mood was buoyant and hopeful, her mind occupied with what she was going to say to Carey and what she prayed he would say to her. In her imagination she saw him as she had when she had first fallen for him, when they had been in the boat that day taking her back to the *Southern Princess*. They had exchanged names and then they had leaned together over her photograph, he looking up from it to test the likeness and examining her features gently, some surprise still in his eyes over the fact that she was the person in it. And later, much later in their acquaintance-ship, she relived that night at Foxholme when he had stood at her bedside darkly handsome in the plain white shirt. Whatever age they had lived in he would have captured her heart. She remembered the rapture and ecstasy that had been hers when their lips had met in passion after he had asked her to marry him. Heaven had smiled on her, but then a few hours later, hell had taken its place.

10

In very little time it seemed Stella reached the ferry terminal and pulled up behind the small queue of cars. She then joined a few people looking out over the terminal wall at activity along the side of the lake. Men were busy pulling *Fair Wind* up on to the beach clear of the water, using a tractor and with ropes attached to its hull. Stella watched dispassionately knowing that Carey was safe, and without him the yacht meant nothing. The thought of the joy awaiting her when at last she found him had kept her going the night before, but things hadn't worked out. Now she was hopeful again.

Once across on the other side of the lake however her mood of regained cheerful optimism began to fade. Her intended mission to Foxholme did not appear quite so appealing as it had done within the sheltering walls of the inn, and in the first glow of the new born idea.

Drawing up outside Foxholme she saw that the large gates were closed, and to her they represented the barrier that existed between herself and Carey. On her last visit, the day of the house party, they had been wide in welcome. Leaving her car and pushing them partly open, she began to make her lonely and apprehensive way up the drive. The house might have been empty with not a window open and the front door closed.

Stella's finger wavered in front of the bell, then pressed it tentatively — there was no turning back now. Doubts now unleashed themselves upon her. She hadn't an idea as to what she was going to say, but she was determined to stay calm and dignified when he appeared and take her cue from his manner.

The door opened and Florence the housekeeper stood there. Recognition came almost instantly and with great surprise. 'Miss Bardon, oh Miss Bardon,' she sighed hugely, bending forward in excited welcome. 'I tried to phone you last night with a message to say that he had been found and was coming home.'

'Thanks, but I met him last night after I had decided to come up to Windermere as I was very worried. I should have been on the way when you phoned.' She paused because even though she had only walked up the drive, she was breathless. 'Is Mr Ganton in?'

'Yes, he is dear, come in and, oh, I was so glad when he was all right,' she said with great relief, closing the door behind them. Then the housekeeper motioned Stella to stand with her in front of the hall window. There she spoke anxiously and in low tones to the younger woman. 'I'm worried about Mr Ganton. He's not himself at all. I know it must have been a shock losing his boat, but . . . ' She stopped and shrugged until her usually cheery face rested apparently without neck upon her shoulders. 'He's not the gentleman I know — snapped at me and been upstairs most of the time.' She looked puzzled as she continued, 'Then I wanted to phone you again today to let you know he was safe and he wouldn't let me.' Stella guessed why and the news did not make her any more confident about her coming meeting with Carey, and the chance of reconciliation.

'And I thought I was settled here,' went on Mrs Preston. 'I really liked working for him.'

Stella was puzzled. 'Has Mr Ganton asked you to leave?'

'Oh no, but he's selling the house. He told me today.'

Cold suddenly clutched Stella's inner being. 'S — selling Foxholme?'

The housekeeper nodded wide-eyed. 'Yes, there's something awfully wrong I'm sure. He's been on the phone already today to the estate agents, I heard him. He's going to do his best to find me another position but I was so happy here.'

Stella wasn't listening. The shock of the news that Carey was leaving Foxholme had set her mind struggling. Was it because of their quarrel? Or was she wrong in thinking that their affair had meant so much to him? And where was he going? A new fear came over her. Was he going back to America? If he did she might never see him again. Stella became aware that Mrs Preston was addressing her again. 'I'm sorry Miss Bardon, I'm keeping you, but I just had to talk to someone. I'll tell Mr Ganton you're here. I'm sure that will cheer him up.'

Watching the older woman mount the stairs to the gallery she was now very doubtful. Standing in the hall alone she felt like an interloper. She heard Florence knock, then a man's muffled voice and the housekeeper announcing her arrival. A few moments later Florence came down into the hall again. 'I've told him, Miss Bardon, I just hope you can do something for him,' then passed Stella, shaking a worried head to disappear into the kitchen.

Stella stood there waiting and gazing at the stairs. Where was the welcome, the racing footsteps and Carey's face and arms bringing forgiveness? Real doubts began to assail her as to the wisdom of calling on him that morning. There came the sound of a door opening and steps on the gallery, then silence as if the person had stopped. With a thumping heart Stella moved further into the hall.

Carey was standing, one hand on the bannister, looking down on her. She couldn't see his expression clearly because of his back being to the gallery window. A smile formed quickly on her lips. She loved him and whatever happened yesterday was over — this was another day. Carey remained silent, and Stella watched as he came down-stairs with slow and deliberate steps. Her brain was already making excuses for him. It was the surprise at her coming that had taken words away from him. He turned at the foot of the stairs to face her, clean shaven and wearing a cream polo neck sweater and dark trousers.

She took a pace towards him eagerly. Soon his face would break into that slow smile she had known and remembered so well.

He stopped. 'I thought that we hadn't anything left to say to each other. I'm sure that I made that clear to you yesterday. As far as I'm concerned everything's over between us.' The words were uttered in an expressionless, matter of fact way.

Stella's gaze remained on him, staggering mentally under the realisation that he did not want to know her any more.

'Why did you come here, Stella? Did you really think a personal visit would make a difference?'

She stared at him dully, quite unable to mask her hurt and despair. He was calm — too calm. Better that he had been angry; a chance for her when the fires had burnt out. 'Yes,' she said simply in a tremulous whisper trying to gather herself from the shattered remnants of her erstwhile hope. It was all so terrible. 'I loved you and you loved me or you said so. You did ask me to marry you — remember?'

'Yes, I remember,' and just for a fraction his face softened, but then his voice hardened with a controlled anger running through his words. 'I also remember two days ago when you wanted nothing to do with me. You didn't want me then so why this sudden change of attitude? You couldn't take me on trust could you and give me a chance to explain? No, you damn well thought the hell of me at the first opportunity.'

'All right, I made a mistake.' Stella snapped her admission. 'But you had no right practically to ignore me last night at the inn.'

'If it hadn't been for you I shouldn't

have been there at all,' he retorted angrily.

'It's not my fault if you go off in a temper and sail a yacht when no-one in their right mind would attempt it.'

'Well you can have what's left of it. I shall not need it — I'm returning to the States.'

'America! You're going back!' and she couldn't keep the alarm out of her voice. If he left England there would be little hope of her seeing him again. A cynical mocking demon told her that even if he stayed there would be little chance of that.

'Yes, I am, Stella,' he said very deliberately while regarding her distantly. 'And you're quite right, I wasn't in my right mind when I took *Fair Wind* out, but I realise now that the whole thing just wasn't worth getting upset about. I just don't care what you think of me, then or now; it's not important.' He smiled without humour, thinly, and added, 'I wouldn't worry about me too much. There'll be other yachts for you to look pretty on.'

His cruel inferences sank into her like the repeated stabs from a dagger. Stick out a thumb and hitch a sail from another yachtsman — preferably a rich one. Stella's world collapsed for the second time in twenty four hours, and so did her determination to remain calm and dignified. Wrong once she may have been, but she wasn't going to remain silent under his rude and insulting remarks. Her Yorkshire spirit rose fiercely in defiance, her frank blue eyes like twin rapiers cleaving the space between herself and the man opposite. She fought to keep her voice strong against the emotions threatening to reduce it to an incoherent hoarseness. 'Well, let me tell you something, Mr Carey Ganton. I don't fall out of love so easily as you appear to do. I loved you — you were superman to me. I used to think how could I be so lucky.' Contempt showed in her expression and tone. 'But not any more because I don't think you could stay in love with

anyone for more than a few hours
— you're too fond of yourself.' She
gulped a breath, then plunged on,
'Anybody as fickle in love as you are
doesn't deserve to be loved. I nearly
died yesterday thinking what might
have happened to you. Did you stop to
think why I was at the inn? It was
because I cared enough to drive up here
as soon as I heard the news. I'd been
working all day, I was tired, but I drove
like mad and spent hours looking for
you, and yet when I found you you
hadn't even the damn manners to be
nice to me, and in front of all those
people. So you'd had a rough time, well
so had I.' Stella's contempt became
even more marked. 'And what were you
doing all the time at the inn? Hitting
the bottle and all because I got mad at
you, and there was I thinking you'd
been drowned. I was upset that night
after the swim when you told me you'd
been married. But what did you expect?
I said things — all right, were they so
unforgivable?' Stella stepped back from

him. 'Anyway, I'll get over you. Run away and take your damn yacht with you. You should have drowned in it.' Her voice finally weakened, suddenly aghast at what her fierce anger had just led her to say.

Carey was making small shaking movements of his head as she finished. Everything between them was ruined. Two adults reduced to trading insults between each other.

Without warning Carey acted swiftly, sweeping her up into his arms and moving towards the door. He had flung it open and they were outside before she recovered herself, wriggling violently to make him release her.

'Put me down, you imbecile,' she choked at him, and the house receded as he marched with a determined and resolute crunch of his feet on the gravel down the drive towards the gates. This couldn't be, her brain said. This was a nightmare to end all nightmares.

Reaching the gates, Carey deposited her on her feet on the path outside.

'Now, Miss Bardon,' he said, 'perhaps you can cool off,' and with that he turned, shutting the gate on her.

Blindly she fumbled with the door of her car, and drove off, unable to see the change that came over Carey, nor to hear his shout for her to come back. At home total humiliation flooded Stella's being. The second visit to Foxholme had been a disaster — an unmitigated disaster. She had been a complete and utter idiot to think that he would welcome her coming to the house. Where had been her pride? She had made herself look cheap, and had been treated accordingly. How could she even have considered the idea? She should have known better, had only herself to blame. If she had listened to Teresa's advice and had left Carey for a few days and then contacted him, things might have been different.

Nevertheless Stella sat brooding and seething with anger. He had treated her badly and his conduct had been thoughtless and selfish. He had dismissed her from his house and life as if she had been some common tramp. He had deserved what she had said to him. She had no regrets over that and gained a bitter satisfaction from the thought.

At about six o'clock that evening the telephone rang, startling her out of her dark mood. She recognised the voice as Carey's and slammed the phone down. The unbelievable ego and cheek of the man. She wouldn't speak to him again if he was the last man on earth. Sunday morning another call from Carey, and she told him that he must have got the wrong number, and that she didn't know anyone of that name.

When she returned home from school the next day a huge bunch of red roses encased in a wrapper awaited her on the doorstep. Stella glanced at the card attached, and did not even bother to read the short message above it. Flinging the package away savagely, she sat down and wept broken heartedly. Red roses — the emblem of love between man and woman. In her case they signified a love she once thought was hers, but now she could no longer risk the heartache by getting involved again. Also her injured pride and a simmering anger barred the way to the love for him that she still held deep inside her.

11

The weeks went by and autumn returned. She received a letter from her sister now based in Australia and working as an airline stewardess. In the letter she went on to suggest that Stella threw up her job as a teacher and go and live in Australia with her. Stella was glad to know that Pauline had found work and was well. Pauline's suggestion that she should join her in Australia was very tempting. It would mean a clean break from the surroundings and memories that brought Carey so easily to mind. And yet . . .

Stella stayed on in Halford in familiar surroundings, perhaps because the idea that she and Carey might meet again had not been completely eradicated from her mind. Even when she had quarrelled with him life had contained an excitement and everything had been in sharper focus. The life she now led was lack-lustre and boring, and to her friends she felt that she must be the same.

The way she was conducting her life she would end up with no friends at all. But the truth was that she had been touched by a searing love and the scars had not yet healed fully. What she ought to do was empty her mind of every thought which had any connection with Carey. Only then would another man have a chance of taking his place.

Stella cursed herself for being weak but the anger and bitterness she had held had begun to fade and at times she found herself thinking of him in a more understanding and kindly way. He had phoned her twice and had sent flowers, yet she had ignored the extended hand of reconciliation. But wasn't that the very attitude that had hurt her so much when he had behaved in the same way towards her? Since the two phone calls and the sending of the flowers there had been no more communication from him. She couldn't have expected anything else. He was lost to her forever and the sooner she got that firmly impressed on her mind the better.

Yet despite this self-lecturing, Stella dialled Foxholme one evening. There was just the chance that he might still be there, and it was possible that it had not yet been sold. A man's voice answered, one that she did not recognize, the speaker informing her that he was the caretaker until the house was sold, and he had no idea where Mr Ganton had gone.

Stella put the phone down, an emptiness pervading her. So that was that. The final act in a chapter of her life. The latter was supposed to be a teacher — though a cruel and hard one at times. What had she learned? Only that love was a delicate thing, flowering strongly in the sunlight of passion, but withering swiftly in the dark and mist of doubt and distrust. She had blundered about in its garden treading on the shoots of love.

The autumn nights were getting longer and on arriving home from work, Stella would usually draw the curtains and sit with a book or watch television. She found it difficult to concentrate on either, but they were ways of diverting her thoughts from the man who had like a comet come close for a fraction of time, and had then vanished from her world.

Then one Friday evening she switched on to view a film. About half way through it Stella became aware that one of the leading supporting roles was being played by someone she thought she'd seen before somewhere. His face was familiar and reminded her of someone she had met.

When the film was over she remained staring keenly at the list of characters and the names of actors playing them. Suddenly she saw it — Kindon Ferrers — Carey's friend who had joined the party on *Fair Wind* on that spring weekend which now seemed so long ago.

Later that night Stella sat curled in her chair drifting in memory. She wondered if Carey had told him about their quarrel. Kindon must have wondered where she had disappeared to when she did not appear for breakfast that morning at Foxholme after she had made her hasty and angry departure. Stella remembered the conversation she and Kindon had had together that afternoon on the boat when he had spoken about his friend. Kindon had mentioned a woman who had been in Carey's life beforehand, but had omitted to say that she had been married to him and had died. Stella sighed deeply. If only Kindon had mentioned that during their conversation, things could have been so different between herself and Carey.

Her thoughts ran on. Where was Kindon Ferrers now? And did he see much of Carey, she wondered? Somewhere in her subconscious an idea was beginning to nudge for recognition, and soon it was forcing itself on to her until she could no longer ignore it. What was to stop her from getting in touch with Kindon Ferrers and finding out if he knew where Carey was? If the actor did know, then she could write to Carey and hope for the best.

The idea was exciting and optimism flared briefly. She had nothing to lose and everything to gain including, she realised, another bout of heartache if things didn't work out. But Stella told herself that it was now up to her to make an attempt at healing the rift between Carey and herself. The trouble was that weeks had elapsed since he had tried to get in touch with her by means of the phone and flowers. Time had gone by and he might have forgotten about her, and could even have fallen in love with someone else. Nevertheless, Stella, driven by the idea, thrust those thoughts aside and discovered that Kindon Ferrers was filming in the south of England near Dorchester.

Getting in touch with him personally was even harder. At one stage she felt that it was just not worth the trouble, with no guarantee that more misery and despair would not be at the end of her quest. But she clung on stubbornly and decided to telephone the main hotels in Dorchester. There would be only a few and she might just get a clue as to which one he was staying at. The depressing thought came that he could be staying some way out of the town, maybe even in one of the coastal resorts some miles away.

But her persistence paid off when she contacted the third hotel on her list. An excited switchboard operator revealed that Kindon Ferrers had been in that hotel with friends for a drink. Then in answer to Stella's urgent plea the operator told her that she had heard he was staying at The Pines Country Hotel near Blandford Forum.

Immediately afterwards Stella wrote to the actor feeling that it was one of the most important letters in her whole life. In it she told him of what had happened between Carey and herself.

She tried to make sure that he remembered her by reminding him that she had met him on *Fair Wind* when he had joined the party as a guest of Carey's earlier in the year. When she had sealed the envelope, Stella wrote her name and address on the back of it and marked it private with deeply indented letters. When he did see the envelope the name might just jog his memory and make him read the contents. She had thought of telephoning but doubted whether she would be allowed to speak to him directly. So many women must do that, claiming to be a friend or someone he had met.

On posting the letter a flicker of hope rose in her, but she told herself not to expect too much, and she uttered a prayer that the sentiments expressed in the message might reach beyond Kindon and touch the man she still loved, wherever he was in the world.

A few days later Stella received a reply, which was brief and brought overwhelming relief to her. Of course he would meet her, and certainly he remembered her, and if he could sort out anything for her he would do so with pleasure. Would she please ring his hotel to verify the day of arrival — weekend would be better for him. She rang immediately to leave a message that she would be arriving at the hotel on the coming Saturday in the late afternoon.

By the time she reached The Pines Hotel she was feeling both nervous and excited. Nervous at the prospect of meeting the actor again, and excited by the fact that he represented a stepping stone to Carey. On her arrival she was informed that Kindon had requested that she meet him in the restaurant at seven thirty. Would he be able to help her or was her journey going to be a waste of time?

The head waiter led her to a corner table more privately positioned where Kindon Ferrers was waiting for her, maroon jacketed, stone coloured trousers and bow tie. He stood up smiling his welcome and took her extended hand.

'Nice to see you again, Stella,' and she noticed his swift appraisal of her.

'It's very good of you to spare the time, Mr Ferrers.'

'Kindon, please, we're not strangers.' When they were seated he said, 'I guessed you might like a little time to yourself after travelling before we met.'

How thoughtful of him; she had appreciated it. 'Thanks Kindon, I was a bit tired,' she admitted, 'but I feel fresher now. I've tidied up.'

Kindon eyed her a moment. 'You look quite delightful,' he stated simply, and she felt it was a genuine compliment and was flattered. If only it had been Carey opposite her and saying that. Would her prayers be answered through Kindon?

Her companion had picked up the menu, looked at her over its top. 'I thought that you might be hungry after the journey. Will you join me for dinner?'

Stella accepted the offer gratefully thinking that most women would have given anything to be dining with the man sat opposite. If it had not been for the tension and anxiety over Carey she herself could have enjoyed the evening more fully.

Although grateful and appreciative of Kindon's kindness, the food was of secondary importance even though she was hungry. Stella was impatient to discuss how he could help her contact Carey, but refrained from broaching the matter just then and instead tried to appear interested in her companion's life and latest work.

For a while he was content to answer her questions and enlarge upon what he had been doing. He was busy on the new film, and when it was finished he was hoping to take a long holiday. Kindon refilled her glass and then leaned forward across the table. 'Much as we actors like to talk about ourselves, the fact is you have come down here to ask for my help in a much more serious matter.' The boyish smile had faded being replaced by a reflective frown. Shaking his head he sighed briefly. 'I'm sorry about you and Carey. I thought you had it made and I was real surprised when I received your letter, Stella. I'd always thought a wedding was imminent and expected an invitation any time.'

Stella smiled sadly at him and nodded. 'It was, then everything went wrong. I'm partly to blame I know, because when I discovered he was married I went to pieces with the shock. After all he'd asked me to marry him only a few hours before, and of course I didn't know that she'd died. I don't think he meant to tell me but we quarrelled again and he lost his temper.' She smiled with a sad wryness at Kindon. 'We only knew each other for a short time and yet we quarrelled several times. It seemed to me beyond the law of averages.'

Kindon nodded, eyeing her with a mixture of sympathy and admiration, then said, 'You must have something Stella. I've never known Carey quarrel with a woman before. He never let it get that far.'

'I was stupid,' observed Stella, 'lost in my hurt pride. He tried to phone me and sent me flowers after the last quarrel but I ignored him.'

'Yes,' commented Kindon, 'between you you've certainly made a mess of what could have been a beautiful friendship, although I have thought that it was perhaps partly my fault.'

She was surprised. 'Your fault? How?'

'Well,' said Kindon, 'I remember talking to you on the yacht that day at Windermere, and I thought then what a great couple you'd make. I didn't want to spoil anything and I felt it wasn't my business to tell you that he'd been married.' He shrugged slightly. 'But then again perhaps if I'd told you then you wouldn't have quarrelled, you'd have known the facts and been prepared.'

'Not at all, Kindon, please don't

blame yourself for any of it. We were two adult people and I should have known better — been more tolerant.'

Her companion shrugged heavily and moved his hands apart. 'Did Carey tell you anything about her?'

'No, nothing apart from the fact that she had died. He was too angry at the time and I didn't want to know any more.'

Kindon studied her for a moment. 'Well, he met her at one of those promotional gatherings. She had been a model — you know the sort of thing. They drape themselves over cars, boats, anything to attract the attention of the would-be buyer. Then she couldn't get work on account of some illness she'd contracted. She'd done some work for Carey's firm before and he was very sorry for her, I know by the way he used to talk to me about her. Anyway to cut a long story short he paid all her medical bills and the doctors told him she wouldn't last long, but the problem was that she'd fallen for him.' Kindon paused as if gathering his thoughts, then went on, 'About a week before she died she asked him if they could be married. Now you've got to understand, Stella, that inside Carey there's a lot of warmth and sympathy. And he just couldn't say no to her. So a priest was brought in and they were married. I think she died a day or so later.'

Poor Carey, thought Stella regretting now more than ever the things she had said to him during their quarrels.

Kindon sipped at his wine then cradled the glass in his hand. 'I didn't see much of him after that for a while — he took himself off on his yacht somewhere. I believe that's where you came in,' added Kindon smiling.

'Yes, that's where it all started,' she affirmed sadly, and didn't need any reminding having played the mental cassette of her life since then over and over again.

Kindon's gaze had sharpened on her, his expression deeply serious, and he spoke slowly as if to give more authority to his words. 'I've known Carey a long time on and off, and you have to believe me, Stella, when I tell you that he didn't love that girl. He was sorry for her, that's all.' The actor paused then continued with great conviction, 'Carey told me the marriage was never consummated and I believed him.'

Stella felt that it was the truth. And in any case what had happened in Carey's life before she met him did not matter.

Kindon refilled her glass, she feeling that he was slightly embarrassed and also in a way relieved that he had said his piece. This impression was confirmed when after refilling his own he said, 'There now I've done my bit for Carey.'

'And very well too, and I appreciate your telling me,' she said gratefully.

He waved her thanks aside. 'Only too pleased. The problem now is how are we going to get you two together again?' Stella couldn't resist asking, 'Do you know where he is?'

'Not exactly. As far as I know he's still head of Sunside yachts. A few calls should locate him.'

And even when Kindon had found him again, what was she going to do? Send a letter? He might ignore it. Phone him? But then there was the risk that he would hang up on her. So what alternatives were left? A challenge must be thrown down to Carey — yes or no. A final gamble on her part in the casino of love. An idea flitted across her mind — an idea so preposterous and bizarre that at first she could not even consider it, but it persisted. It was all or nothing for her.

She became aware that Kindon was observing her. 'Sorry Kindon, I was lost in thought. I've got an idea. With your help it might just work for me.'

Kindon heard the hopeful optimism and saw the strain in the frank blue eyes of the young woman across the table. 'Sure Stella, you've got it. Just tell me what you have in mind.'

She did with an earnest enthusiasm,

then stared at him expectantly. 'Well, what d'you think?'

Kindon gazed at her in wonderment. 'What do I think? It's crazy — completely crazy — more like a film script.' He must have seen the despair creeping into her eyes. 'No, no, I'm not turning it down. It may just be the way to play it. What was that date again?'

Stella gave it to him. 'You're a real friend in need Kindon,' she said with great feeling.

'Well, I can't promise, but it won't be for want of trying on my part.'

'Some day I might be able to help you,' she said.

'You can now,' and Kindon's eyes danced at her. 'You can reserve me a front pew in the church at your wedding.'

Stella chuckled with as near happiness as she had felt for a long long time. 'Nothing would please me more.' She felt a hundred per cent better for her meeting with Kindon, and the fact that he had agreed to help, then wondered whether he would be working in the morning. That would be Sunday, but you never knew with actors, and she did not wish to outstay her welcome, and also she had a long drive to face. 'I think I'd better go soon, Kindon.'

Kindon made space for his elbows on the table. 'Look, I hope you don't mind Stella, but I've booked a room for you overnight. I guessed you wouldn't be at school tomorrow and it's a long way to travel in the dark.'

Stella stared back at him. The evening had contained surprises. She was glad and relieved. 'It's very kind and thoughtful of you Kindon.' She had as a precaution brought overnight things with her in the car just in case she had a breakdown, and had also brought enough money.

'Well, Carey wouldn't think much of me if I didn't take care of you,' Kindon pointed out.

Perhaps Carey didn't care by now anyway, and for a moment the thought dampened Stella's new-found hopeful optimism.

Not long afterwards she prepared to say goodbye to Kindon. The actor had said he may be on the set in the morning and would probably be gone before she arose. He waved aside her attempt to reimburse him for the cost of the room.

'Invite me to the wedding. That will be enough for me.'

If only she could feel so confident that all would be well. 'You know you'll be the first,' she smiled cheerfully nevertheless. Suddenly stark anxiety showed. 'You won't forget Kindon, will you? November the fifteenth.'

Kindon took her by the hand and patted it and said reassuringly, 'Don't worry, Stella. I wouldn't forget because I know just what it means to you.'

Stella leaned forward and kissed him on the cheek. 'You're a wonderful person and thanks for everything. Goodnight, Kindon.'

For a man who as an actor must have

kissed hundreds of women, and been kissed by them, that particular peck upon Kindon Ferrers' cheek appeared to give him an inordinate amount of pleasure.

As she lay in bed afterwards the date November the fifteenth was emblazoned in her mind and in her heart. A very special date to come in the near future. Perhaps the most important day of her life.

12

Just after dawn that day Stella stood on the beach of the island where she had first met Carey, watching the launch which had brought her disappearing from sight. Was the plan crazy? Maybe she was, she thought, surveying the otherwise empty horizon. It was the biggest gamble she would ever make all her life, but if when that boat returned she and Carey stepped aboard, then what she had done would have been worth that desperate gamble. Had Kindon Ferrers succeeded in tracing Carey and passing on her message to him? The message being for him to meet her on the island on that day the fifteenth of November when she would be waiting for him. A fervent and earnest prayer had winged along with it.

She began to walk along the beach wondering whether she was just being a fool, her heart ruling her reason. She was jeopardising her job by making excuses to have time off, and had dipped deeply into her bank savings for the trip. Supposing Carey did not come there would be further heartbreak and the real possibility of a breakdown. An emotional high could not be maintained for ever; something would have to give.

Already it was warm but not as hot as that day when she had visited the island from the liner, but of course it had been afternoon then. Stella reached the ridge over which she had first seen Carey, having been drawn to it again, and looked over. It was empty, only the shelter below at the rear of the beach to convince her that it had not just been a dream, and if she had to spend a night alone on the island at least she would have some protection from the cooler night air. Or would, as she had prayed so often for, be enfolded in Carey's arms, willingly smothering in the warmth of his body. Her own turned weak instantly at the thought.

She glanced down at herself, being dressed exactly as she had been on that first visit to the island — in white — wide brimmed hat, half sleeved top and short skirt. She had done it deliberately, Carey having once told her that he had fallen in love with her immediately on seeing her.

From where she stood she could see the waters surrounding the island clearly. But there was no sign of a boat, only the sparkling sea, the birds, and the occasional disturbance made by the splash of a fish. From which direction would Carey come? Would it be from Las Palmas as she had done? *If* he came, a voice mocked inside her.

Midday arrived and no Carey with it. It was hot and she sat in the shade of an umbrella pine staring out over the sea. What confidence and hope she had were now ebbing away fast. She had been utterly stupid, and love had blinded her, to suppose that her message would make him drop everything and race to a small island thousands of miles away.

A noise penetrated her depression — the sound of an aircraft. She scanned the sky with little interest. It was no doubt a holiday plane bound for the Canary Islands. Focusing on it, a dark speck in the blue, she watched it then realised that it was drawing nearer and that it was a helicopter, its clattering sound becoming louder.

Eyes fixed on it she was on her feet swiftly. The craft came swinging in then hovered, disturbing the sand and swaying the branches near her. She could see someone at the controls. Transfixed, Stella saw the figure of a man appear dangling on a rope ladder from the side of the helicopter away from her and silhouetted against the water. As she watched the figure let go of the ladder and fell into the sea, and then the aircraft climbed away and made off into the distance, leaving the man swimming towards the beach.

Stella did not feel the rocky path down to the beach. Wings of love carried her effortlessly. She knew! It was Carey rising out of the water and coming up the beach. Just as she had seen him the first time. A new start. Sobbing with joy she stumbled over the sand to lock against him. Words were beyond them — they would come later. He had come — he had come — he loved her!

Gently yet passionately Carey lifted her and with their lips joined carried her into the shade of the shelter.

* * *

To complete the miracle that Stella had asked for they were married in Hawkshead Church before Christmas, and a delighted Kindon Ferrers was the best man.

Afterwards Carey took his bride to live at Foxholme and at Stella's request he reinstated a happy Florence to run the kitchen again. And that first night as they lay entwined Stella sighed contentedly. They too had been reinstated in each other's hearts.

VISIONS OF THE HEART

Christine Briscomb

When property developer Connor Grant contracted Natalie Jensen to landscape the grounds of his large country house near Ashley in South Australia, she was ecstatic. But then she discovered he was acquiring — and ripping apart — great swathes of the town. Her own mother's house and the hall where the drama group met were two of his targets. Natalie was desperate to stop Connor's plans — but she also had to fight the powerful attraction flowing between them.

DIVIDED LOYALTIES

Phyllis Demaine

When Heather's fiancé, Adrian, is offered a wonderful job in America their future seems rosy. However, Adrian's brother, Carl, a widower, asks for Heather's help with his small, deaf son. Help which, as a speech therapist, Heather is qualified to give. But things become complicated when Carl goes abroad on business and returns with Gisel, to whom his son takes an instant dislike. This puts Heather in the position of having to choose between the boy's happiness and her own.